HARD WAY
TO HAPPINESS

HARD WAY TO HAPPINESS
(A SOLDIER'S HISTORY)

RAYNAND

Kravitz & Sons

INNOVATORS IN PUBLISHING, MARKETING AND ADVERTISING

Kravitz and Sons LLC
1301 Farmville Blvd, Suite 104
Greenville, NC 27834

Published by Kravitz and Sons LLC.

ISBN: 979-8-89639-243-9   (sc)
ISBN: 979-8-89639-244-6   (e)

Library of Congress Control Number: 2025907347

In tribute to General Jay B Silveria, soldier

and man of courage,

to honor him for his speech on September 28, 2019 at

US Air Force Base Academy.

In memory of the late John Sidney McCain III,

Soldier, Congressman, Senator, and Man of honor.

For what he stands for best as a true American.

Table of Contents

America is an incredible country. It is, perhaps, the only one on this planet that today represents the true face of the United Nations. In New York City, you can meet, at least, an immigrant from every continent and every country in the world. If the native Indians are the only true owners of this land but after the proclamation of the independence in 1776, America had become more than a nation of immigrants, but an idea symbolized by its constitution, its flag, and its diversity. The bills of rights, the civil war, the end of slavery, the fight for civil rights, and recently the Black Lives Matter movement keep changing this country.

The United States Army, over the years, has become the symbol and image of this ideal with roughly the same diversity of cultures, religions, races, and beliefs. It is the only institution, despite the progress it still has to make, to accept differences of origin and social class to the point of creating links basically based on belonging to a team, submission to a hierarchy, and obedience to a code.

This book is the history of this America. Of this soldier who is, at the same time, Captain John McCain, General Jay B. Silveria, and Chief of Staff Colin Powell. That is him who will overcome the last barriers of racial discriminations to push the American values to the point of becoming the frontline of the most perfect human civilization.

CHAPTER 1
A Brutal Awakening

Earlier this morning in that day of September 30, 1991, Port-au-Prince, the Haitian capital was in a boil. A chaotic and confusing situation developed downtown as the sun rose. Independent radios already reported that several dozens of people would have been killed.

Ray Gaillard was still nonchalantly sleeping in his bed despite the fact that he had been informed by a CIA agent, from the American Embassy, to remain alert because the army is braced for several days for a possible overthrow of the government. In this residential area, crested in Belleville, where he lived since his return to Haiti, the deployment of military forces engaged in a coup against President Jean Bertrand Aristide did not arrive until then. Although he had good contacts within the army, he had been advised not to show his nose outside since a large part of the staff did not appreciate that he alerted the government to the conspiracy in preparation. Indeed, he had, in an article that appeared in a newspaper a week ago, announced the military coup with eminently pointing details of the death threats he had been receiving. His future brother-in-law, a highranking army officer of the Port-au-Prince police force, the nerve of the conspiracy, had told him that he was a target. It was necessary to silence this annoying witness who had evidence that in addition to the technical support of the CIA, the aficionados helped out from the funding of some rich people and Colombian drug dealers notoriously known.

Ray got to the idea that by publishing this article, although he wasn't a supporter of this populist president, that the American Government was going to think twice before authorizing an act of military insubordination that would break the fragile democratic momentum. He wanted to reconcile his responsibilities as an American patriot and his love for his country of origin.

Ray was a former US Army Special Forces officer, a Haitian origin belonging to the famous Navy Seal, under cover of United States Agency for International Development (USAID) but worked, in fact, for the Drug Enforcement Administration (DEA) for two years. He was responsible for spying the Latin American Division and the Caribbean on drug trafficking and money laundering which were involved in the military, members of the government, and the banking sector in particular. He was a dandy who impressed both opponents and fervent supporters of the new president. He had his entry into the popular circles of the organization's employer, workers, and political parties by facilitating access to funds arranged by the CIA and DEA through the program monitoring of organizations of civil society managed by USAID. Thus, he had been able to infiltrate the key elements of the traffic and its ramifications both in the banks that laundered the money as in some Haitian embassies and South America loaded of the transfer through diplomatic couriers. Military, musicians, government members, and reputable businessmen were taking advantage of the traffic, sometimes knowledgeable CIA that protected its own information corridors both in Haiti and in some Latin American countries.

Since his arrival at Port-au-Prince for over two years, Ray had used his military history to establish strong relationships with the Haitian army at all levels from the bottom up to the hierarchy. He had offered free expertise both at the military academy and at the training center for recruits of Fort Lamentin camp. He endorsed, quite often, a military member of the consulate to obtain a visa for himself, his wife, and even children. And finally, he offered occasionally small gifts to each other to maintain the friendship. He was an excellent agent and a man with real popularity in the popular organizations and political parties, all tendencies combined.

His first meeting with Sarah was quite a good luck. That night, he was investigating a Colombian drug dealer who came to establish contacts with relatives of the newly elected president. The political power had changed hands; it was necessary to ensure the political and judicial protection of the traffic through those who controlled the political power of the country since the army having already secured its share of the work. In this chic Pétion-Ville restaurant, he was a loyal customer, so no one should suspect his presence as a spy job. It took very little time to identify this Colombian little discreet who commanded the best dishes and the more expensive drinks. The Haitians were bragging about it, aloud of their influence, and that it was with them and not with the military that the drug dealer had to deal with. Ray registered everything, sitting on chair close by its neighbors, at the very least, arrogant, pretending to be lost in the documentary broadcast at national television on the case of Manuel Antonio Noriega, the former strong man of Panama.

This night, Sarah Altieri and her big brother, Lt. Col. Fred Joseph Altieri, had dinner with friends from the American Embassy. The soldier was a spy's recruit of the National Security Agency (NSA), the powerful intelligence agency of the US Army, since his first internship at Fort Bragg. At the time, he was a young officer from a humble family with no future and no protection. He was assigned without a spare in all the bad parts of the country. But after being recruited by the NSA, everything changed. He immediately had a new good assignment at the police headquarter to the point of being solicited during all military coups that saw an officer spilled another until the election of the current president. Due to lack of the political stability of military governments, the American administration decided to put an end to this situation which threatened the foundations of an army they needed to maintain order in Haiti. So the State Department and US Embassy needed him as a trusted man. Since then, he had climbed the ladder faster than others with advantages that his comrades envied in silence.

It was on leaving the toilets that they had encountered violently against each other. Ray was a tough 240 pounds for 2 meters in height while Sarah was 150 pounds for 1.65 meters. The girl lost the balance and found herself on the ground. Ray rushed to her to help her rise, but she could not move her right foot, and a sudden pain made her grow a cry which attracted the attention of the restaurant manager. Ray carried her in his arms to the table of her brother who felt it urgent to drive her to the hospital. Ray and the colonel had not called the medical emergency. It was not worth it. There was never any available for the living. They had decided to drive the young woman themselves at the hospital. Once she was in the hands of the doctor, the two men took the opportunity to get acquainted and to talk about the political situation. They found really common points and several reasons to meet together later. But Ray already knew him for a long time. He knew also his level of involvement in drug traffic and how he was protected by the NSA. But he was that soldier who carried out orders and who, in return, received little advantage from a system that paid off big at his commanders and others better off than him. So Ray decided to make a friend, if not an ally.

Ray insisted on paying Sarah's medical bill and proposed to take care of her during the convalescent period. Indeed, the latter led him every day at work in the morning and returned to fetch her in the afternoon. He accompanied her to the church every Sunday although he was an atheist. For the next three months, they became real friends, a friendship that had been quickly transformed into a passionate and official affair. They got engaged twelve months later with a promise to be married on the second Saturday of October. They could not imagine that the army would decide to change their project fifteen days before the scheduled date.

This morning of September 30, 1991, Ray Gaillard still stretched on his bed when the phone rang. Colonel Fred was at the end of the line. He said without politeness, "I do not have time to explain you. Get out of your home right now."

"What?" Ray replied, circumspect.

"Get out now, fucking shit! They're already on their way to kill you. Take your passport and especially your handgun, you'll need it. Good luck!" And he hung up.

Ray hurried to the cupboard and removed the hatch which hid a drawer, taking a Beretta and the twelve chargers. He charged it and advanced as soon a bullet was in the collar. He dressed in his blue jeans containing multiple pockets and a green T-shirt on which he wore with his waistcoat by bullets. Then he grabbed the shirt he wore usually when he went to training at a military academy that hid the gun. The other eleven shippers— as well as his passport, purse, credit card, and cash— were scattered throughout his many left pockets and right at knee height. Hardly, he had finished wearing his hat when he heard the rowdy voice of his fiancée in the parlor. She was talking hardly to the guardian who insisted she should go home without any further delay. She didn't want to hear anything. She believed that the function of her brother in the army could protect her from any danger especially since this was also in the conspiracy of the coup. When she rushed angrily into the room, Ray was about to get out, and they almost collided like the evening at the restaurant. With all her anger, she hit the newspaper on the chest of her fiancé. What is that shit? How can you dare do this to me! Then she began by vehemently reproaching him with his lightness and sympathy for this crappy government that raised citizens against each other. In spite of gestures and attempts to calm her, she did not anger.

By trying politely in vain to calm down Sarah without success, Ray lost his composure. He ended up using the strong way by shaking her with strength and cried angrily, "We have to leave this house right now." It was scarcely lost!

For an answer, she drew her engagement ring of his finger and slipped it into her fiancé's pocket. "Now you can marry your mother!" Then she headed toward the exit door of the drawing room. When she set foot on the gallery, she turned her head one last time to watch Ray, tears in her eyes. She did not see the military crossed the fence. She did not have time either to hear this gust of submachine guns that instantly blew her off. Then the military fired all over the house. The second person who had been touched was the guardian. Two men in uniform then entered the maid's room located in the dependence of the courtyard and killed her with at least ten bullets. Even the dog was executed in cold blood. As the windows and doors were targeted with extreme anger, the military sought to surround the house to prevent Ray from retiring. It was absolutely necessary to know that he was out alive. Two Colombian drug dealers, wearing the army uniform for the occasion, were sent to the scene to order the expedition and identify the corpse. It was agreed that after the operation, they had to completely clean the premises and bury the bodies in the mass grave of Titanyen with the numerous others then a bulldozer should cover it an hour later. They were waiting for the Ray's corpse. In the neighborhood, everybody would bury themselves at home, fear in the guts.

Ray responded instinctively after the first gunshots by the military. He removed the screen especially from his Beretta and house to avoid bullets and glass shards that split at his head. When he saw two soldiers penetrated into the living room, he made fire immediately and slaughtered them with one bullet each. He hurriedly turned into the dining room to slaughter the other two who had just crossed the door. The other soldiers turned back and launched three grenades that rolled in the living room before exploding. Ray skirted on the ground and protected the table that still had his breakfast. The explosion made a deafening noise and shattered the windows. Then the soldiers gathered in the street and asked for help. Another patrol was expected to arrive in less than five minutes. Ray knew he had no time at all when he saw the soldiers sought to take a position in the neighboring houses in order to have a view at 380 degrees. It was time for him to counterattack. He seized an M-16 and all the chargers of one of the dead soldiers at hand, reached, and walked to the exit door of the kitchen overlooking the courtyard. Before jumping the wall that gave access to the property at the back of the maid's room, he watered the vicinity of bursts of bullets so indiscriminately. The military didn't expect for this kind of response, and they ran to shelter. He took advantage of the chaos to speed up. Now he knew that the military wanted really to kill him, so he was going to play it hard. He had just awakened his soldier instincts.

CHAPTER 2
THE PURSUIT RACE

Realizing that four of them were dead and five others wounded, the military had become furious. For the first time, they used a bazooka to target home. Then it was a fire of M-1 and M-16, which took the bazooka to be destroyed. When they returned, the interior was a pile of debris. Sarah's unrecognizable body was shredded by explosions of grenades and a bazooka. All the bodies were loaded in a truck, and military set fire to the house. One of the Colombians suggested that the neighborhoods of Vivi Michel, Tabarre, a part of Pétion-Ville, and Delmas were curly. The bodies of the soldiers were transported to the military hospital morgue. Sarah, the guardian, and the servant took the direction of the mass grave in Titanyen with twenty others picked up along the way. One hour later, while the bodies were being buried unsparingly in a common grave, the commander of the Port-au-Prince police announced that an armed commando in the government's pay was caught this morning in a private house in Belleville in the process of preparing a conspiracy. Armed men of this commando fired on a military patrol, killing several people, and wounded among them were innocent soldiers and peaceful citizens. The armed forces, awardee of their duties, started their pursuit so that they would be arrested and handed over to justice for the sequels of law. Thus far, a second message went through radio communication of the army reports of a bonus of $20,000 to be awarded to the patrol that killed Ray. Colombians would take care of the money.

Ray quickly reversed the courtyard after he crossed the wall separating his house from that of the neighbor. Taking the direction of the barrier, he saw a motocross bike in the parking lot at the side of the family vehicle. The driver, who was going to come out, had relented on hearing the detonations and bullets that fell out to his house. He had quickly dropped the bike on the ground with the keys committed in the starter to escape inside. Ray had no problem raising it, starting it, and going away at full speed. On the time for the military to intervene, he had already taken the direction of Bas-de-Delmas using adjacent streets. He had to avoid the neighborhood of Tabarre where the president whose resignation had just been announced lived and the seizure of power by a military junta composed of three senior officers.

The situation on Delmas Road was chaotic. The pavement was filled with debris, barricades, tires inflamed, and cadavers. The army had just suppressed a popular protest that was trying to barricade the artery so to prevent the president from being brought to the airport to be exiled to Venezuela. Women, minors, and especially many members of popular organizations were killed without mercy.

The blood that flowed in the gutters began to dry out with the sun coming up. Ray rode cautiously on the lookout in the midst of this apocalyptic scene. Smoke from burned tires blackened the scenery. Delmas looked like a popular insurrection scene. Ray was unable to see these hidden people behind the walls that tried to tell him to leave the street as long as he was concerned about the brittleness of its situation. By the time he left Delmas Road to obligate on that from the airport, he faced an army patrol that kept the crossroads. The military was waiting for him. At the first opportunity, they opened fire with machine guns without warning. Ray received several bullets in his chest and abdomen, happily stopped by his waistcoat. The bike had been hit in several places. He was thrown back, which unbalanced his conduct. He let the bike fall and slipped to a makeshift shelter. At that point, the military quickly got closer and continued to shoot. He had to react immediately. If he didn't, he would have died in less than thirty seconds. He recovered the M-16 and fired back. The military receded and sought, in their turn, a shelter. Ray took advantage to counterattack. He fired at close range and touched several targets, two of which died on the field. So he stood upright to advance and to fire with his gun without stopping. At that moment, panic won the military. They understood that they faced a professional who was not afraid of anything. They abandoned their two military vehicles to flee in disarray to the bottom of Delmas.

Ray took one vehicle and shot in the right tire of the other. He found in the back seat two M-1, some ammunition, disintegration grenades, and communication radio. He wore a military cap, started the vehicle, and took the road to the airport. He proposed to go to the city of Croix-des-Bouquets, about ten kilometers farther, and then went where there was a checkpoint on the Haitian-Dominican border. He did not know exactly how he would proceed to get to the neighboring territory, but he said to himself that he'd improvise over the course of events.

The road to the airport was completely deserted. Ray rolled at full speed with his mind on alert. Driving an army vehicle, he gave the impression of making a few cases of patrols that circulated the other lane separated by a band of the median. He needed to give the impression to be one of them. As long as a search notice was not launched on the vehicle, he would be able to roll as if it were on an official mission.

The kindliness of those soldiers he crossed on the road to the airport made him suspicious. He believed that something important had just happened. Driven by curiosity, he put on the national radio occupied by the army. It was at that time that Colonel Sylva announced that the president had signed his resignation and that he was exiled to Venezuela. Colonel Sylva said at the same time that instead of a military junta, the new government was delegated to the president of the Supreme Court. The columnist also read a fax he had just received reporting the attack on a military convoy at the level of the crossroads from the airport by a dozen armed supporters of former President Aristide and several military and civilian casualties. This really worried Ray. He was not wrong. Immediately thereafter, a search notice was launched by radio communication against him while he avoided the roundabout to head to the airport. From this crossroads to the starting ramp, corpses were scattered all over the pavement. They were all enthusiast followers of the president coming from the neighborhood of Cite Soleil and other slum surroundings that had tried to oppose the forced departure of the president for exile. Ray was identified in the news as one of the killers on the payroll of the deposited government that was sowing terror in order to cast the stigma on the army. The order was given to immobilize him by any means necessary. The information also reported the description, the vehicle's itinerary, and the driver's identity. While Ray entered at the Carrefour Fleuriot in the direction of the Croix-des-Bouquets, he was chased by two patrols of a dozen soldiers. A chase race with exchanges of gunshots was happening on the usually crowded, but now deserted road full of debris and inflamed tires.

The violent armed confrontation ended inside the city of Croix-des-Bouquets through a series of accidents which immobilized the three vehicles involved in the pursuit. One of the vehicles took fire and exploded shortly after four of the occupants had jumped out avoiding death narrowly. The body of the fifth was fragmented into a thousand pieces with ammunition and the grenades. The three vehicles were recessed in different houses, riddled with bullets. In total, two soldiers were dead and five others wounded. At that moment, a glass-tinted SUV stopped about thirty yards from the scene. Three heavily armed men alighted there in order to check if the driver of the vehicle wanted was dead. They sprinkled it with several bursts of bullets and even launched a grenade. In view of the condition of this vehicle, they had no idea that the driver should have died. But Ray had abandoned the steering wheel immediately after the accident and was hidden behind one wall. Taking advantage of their certainty, he leaped from his hiding place to shoot down the three armed civilians. The soldiers refolded in it profusely. Once he felt out of reach, Ray sat on the SUV and went off at full speed toward the border of Malpasse through a roundabout route. It was no longer recommended to take the paved route that he already knew to be arranged with several checkpoints. Five minutes later, a new alert was launched on the SUV. This time around, thirty soldiers from the western command of the army were launched in pursuit. At the same time, a helicopter flew over the area to facilitate the search.

Ray rolled as soon as possible on this dirt road toward the border in a comfortable vehicle that the owner had changed so that it was really to his taste. When you're a drug dealer, it does not skimp on resources. When he arrived in undergrowth sheltered from the indiscretions possible from the helicopter and from any curious, he parked the vehicle under a tree to inspect the interior. In the back seat, he discovered true arsenal weapons that they would never have in a private vehicle. He found two rifles with glasses long scopes, two M-1, two Ar15, three M-16; a dozen of Magnum 44 and revolvers; observation glasses; ammunition boxes; American, Colombian, and Haitian passports; and boxes of condoms. When he opened the back door, he found further weapons, other ammunitions, and a large military bag bearing the inscription JMF/Port-au-Prince. He opened eagerly, knowing that time was counted for him. He had the surprise of his life. Indeed, he found that there was a huge amount of lots of one hundred American bills. At first glance, it could be between $5 million and $10 million. At the bottom of the bag, he also found American Treasury bonds. He felt that the loot would represent a little more than twelve million. By the time he closed the bag, he heard the purring of the helicopter flying over the area. He followed it with his eyes until he disappeared from his sight. He decided to abandon the vehicle to circumvent the Lake Azuei avoiding the border crossing. Before leaving, he was arming himself in anticipation of new confrontation and hurried the vehicle into the lake. He walked for thirty minutes before crossing the border on foot. Once on the other side, he slipped his weapons in the lake except one Magnum 44 and the corresponding ammunition. With about $30, he paid a Dominican rider who drove him in a short time to the small town closest to the border. From there, he called the chief of the DEA antenna in Santo Domingo who came in person with two of his deputies looking for him in a small helicopter. The latter had been informed by the American Embassy in Port-au-Prince of his situation and his concerns for Ray's life because like the military, he had lost his mark after the confrontations of the Croix-des-Bouquets. Not only was the antenna of the NSA intercepted by the communications of the army, but also its undercover agent, Lt. Col. Fred Joseph Altieri, informed him as the situation progressed.

The DEA agent did not ask him any questions about his bag, merely asking him for an oral report until he wrote it down. At first glance, it could be its personal effects. Ray also had his face marked of emotion. He had just delivered the last great battle of his life. His companions encompassed easily. So there was no question of asking him about details. Once the briefing was over, a long silence was set up while the spacecraft was flying over the verdant landscape of the Dominican Republic. Ray thought of sorrow to his country of origin in the torment and especially of those thousands of people who were already dead and those who were still going to die. As for the president and the members of his government, they were already in the shelter. As always, it was the little people who must pay the tribe of the debacle. Finally, for him, the Haitian adventure was over. He's going to wait until he's in the United States to resign from the DEA and disappear from the radar to get him forgotten. He decided not to risk his life and prepare to start a family.

Ray arrived in Santo Domingo before nightfall. His companion from the DEA dropped him, as he had wished, at the Haitian embassy without delay. His friend, the second consul for six months, was waiting for him. He was also his safest informant within the embassy which was a corridor in the drug trafficking. It was him that passed the traffic information that managed the dealers on both sides of the border. The DEA considered him as a clandestine agent both in the government and in the middle of the drug trade. So he was able to take dividends in return for services rendered.

Ray decided to spend the night at the embassy; it was safer. Two soldiers of the Dominican Army permanently ensured the safety of the outside. He kept his Magnum 44 loaded at dandy, in case. That night, after taking a bath, he passed some calls and went sleeping on a sofa bed at his friend's office making sure everything was fine and closed double turn.

Ray met again his friend early in the morning. They had given rendezvous to discuss his unexpected arrival in Santo Domingo. When he had finished telling him, in part, his journey from Port-au-Prince, he asked him to travel with him to New York to secure by diplomatic briefcase the information holding in his bag but did not breathe a word of its contents. It was a trivial procedure for this one. He was already accustomed to shipping huge amounts of money by this way. He was, therefore, not praying to obtain the safe conduct of his superior. Ray consequently deposited himself the bag in a briefcase bearing the labels: "Diplomatic courier from the Haitian Embassy in Santo Domingo, Dominican Republic, to the Haitian Embassy, New York, United States

America." Then Ray and his friend surrendered at the Las Americas Airport to take a commercial American Airlines flight to John Fitzgerald Kennedy Airport, New York. Before leaving, he gave his friend, in a closed box, his Magnum 44 and the others' passports and asked him never to open it without his permission.

Ray and his friend recovered the briefcase and passed the customs without any problem. When they arrived at the exit of the airport, Brian Donovan was waiting for them. He was his financial agent, the one that managed his investments. He had left the army to get into his father's business on Wall Street. The latter had done the same, as well as his grandfather, a family tradition that he had to honor.

With the money that Ray had accumulated when he left the army including allowances received after his disaffection, he had about $300,000 of funds that grew in risk-free investments. Brian was his trusted man, his former senior officer with whom he was linked with friendship during clandestine operations. They were so related outside even business issues. The question of trust and confidentiality was therefore not with them. Instead, they faced the exit of the arrival room of the airport; they had given themselves a big hug. The phone call he had received from Santo Domingo had frankly worried him. The voice from the line that Brian was heard of was emotional. The Haitian friend of Ray looked impressed because Brian looked like a super banker who came out of a catalog of Goldman Sachs. But the two ex-soldiers did not seem concerned about the sights of the Haitian. After the use of presentations, Ray slipped the diplomatic briefcase in the trunk of Brian's last Cadillac model and proposed to drop off his friend at the Haitian consulate in Manhattan.

Brian brought Ray to his office to talk head-on in the strategy of money laundering and investment and especially the behavior that Ray had to adapt in order not to draw attention to him. He was the one who proposed to him to sell his apartment in West Palm Beach to buy another in the state of Alabama. He advised him to do a low profile by looking for a job and to enroll in the university. Brian suggested even to look after the sale of the apartment in West Palm Beach to get his stuff transferred to wherever he wanted. He had friends in Alabama who could help him settle down. Anyway, Ray didn't have to worry about the details of all these operations. He would take care of it personally.

After that, they had made an agreement, and Ray signed the papers. Brian removed the bag from the diplomatic briefcase and went alone at his bank. What's going to happen didn't concern Ray. He had his own financial network. It was strictly a professional secret. In the evening, they had dinner together, and late at night, it was Brian himself who drove Ray to the airport. A new life awaited him in the state of Alabama.

CHAPTER 3
A NEW BEGINNING

Ray had just left the office of the counselor who was taking care of his registration at the University of Alabama with the certainty of returning to school very soon. As Brian had advised him two months ago, he had bought a small apartment in a peaceful neighborhood of Montgomery, taken a few days of rest, and did his medical checkup before deciding to take over the university at the expense of the army. He had decided not to buy a vehicle but a bicycle for any means of personal transport. Otherwise, he would use the bus like the common citizen.

On that day, the counselor had given him the necessary instructions for his registration for computer and communication class. While he had just got out peacefully from his last interview and would round the corner toward the exit of the building, a pretty young woman fell upon him like a storm. The force of collision projected him on the ground, and she had completely plated on him, butt in the air. As she wore a dress very short, she found herself half naked. The documents she brought under her right arm were mixed with those of Ray. When she realized her uncomfortable situation, she shrieked, at once, with discomfort and pain. Like a good gentleman, Ray fixed on her eyes and presented himself with a bit of humor without realizing that he was bleeding from the head. Instead of answering, the young woman rose promptly and uttered, this time, a horrified cry, disturbed by the sight of the blood flowing abundantly. Before Ray realized it, he had lost consciousness. The young lady became hysterical until she was calmed down by the people alerted by his cries. It was a general panic.

Ray came back at the university hospital of Montgomery four hours later with a horrible headache. He was in intensive care, and his condition, in the beginning, was a lot that worried the doctors, given that he had received a violent shock behind his head when he fell on the floor in the university hallway. When he opened his eyes, the faces that fixed him seemed blurry. Even before he spoke, the first sentence he uttered was to make a caustic joke: "What kind of elephant had I spilled me?"

The nurse was the first to lean courtesy toward him and told him with a big smile, "Since you have regained consciousness and you seem to go better, I leave you with the elephant, and I will get the doctor."

She immediately left the room except for the silhouette of a young White woman who looked embarrassed and completely novice. She bent and turned to him with a pale face, still troubled by the events, and said with a voice soft and confused, "I am Joyce Gallagher, the elephant who had knocked you down."

Joyce watched over Ray out of the emergency room. Given that the latter had no family in this city and that neither the police nor the university had, for the moment, contact with none of his closest relatives, she thought conscientiously that it was up to her to take care of him until his exit of the hospital. Besides, she had promised to the dean of the university to take care and report back to him. The severity of the incident made him hired as the head of a prestigious institution created at the end of the nineteenth century. It was the title to send to the university that she had presented herself and that hospital had allowed him to stay in the room and to provide information on the progress of the patient.

When Joyce got on the bed to talk to Ray, he had his mouth gaping, as he was struck by the beauty of the girl. His face immediately relaxed as if this apparition had calmed the pain he still felt. She gave him an indifferent smile and tried just to be nice as much as possible, neither more nor less. She seemed rather upset to be there. Five hours had passed since the events, and she was stuck there as a result of an unfortunate coincidence. Looking at the expression of his face, Ray had it all figured out. He knew, as a former DEA agent, deciphering facial expression and body language. No sooner, they finished, warmly acquainted with a medical team in the room. The medical team should transport him to another room. Having been informed that Joyce was not of the family, the doctor with the opinion of the patient asked the girl to go and wait for him in the waiting room. She kept silent, not insisted, and she went out without saying a word.

The medical team passed twenty minutes with the patient. She decided to keep him in observation and hang the following twenty-four hours to make a complete medical checkup as well as many x-rays to ensure that there would be no sequelae afterward. The dean of the faculty had called the hospital director to ensure that everything would be done for the patient and that he was treated with the utmost care. In this southern city, people of color did not always get the respect that their case deserved. The NAACP had still a lot to do to make the word equality mean in this kind of institution. Before the medical team left, Ray had asked for a sleeping pill, especially that they didn't let anyone in his room until further notice. It was an embarrassing moment for the doctor who was already on the doorstep. However, he reversed to understand the merits of this request. He explained to the patient that the girl watched over him since his arrival at the hospital and that it would be inappropriate to treat her in this way. "But, Ray, I don't even know that pretty young person."

"Well," answered the doctor, "as you wish." Then he called the nurse to inform him of the query of the patient and went away, looking surprised.

When the doctor left the room of Ray, he had cordially little jumps in the mood of this patient. Besides, he had found it strange that this beautiful young White woman was at the bedside of this Black man. Although this one had turned him down, it was not to please him. But along the corridor, he fell nose to nose on her. She walked up to Ray's room. It was time for her to go home. She wanted to pay tribute to him before leaving and especially for how he would fend. To avoid any misunderstanding, the doctor stopped her road and strove, despite himself, to explain that according to the rules of the hospital, he was obliged to forbid access to the patient's room if she could not justify her links with him. The girl seemed to have received a blow on the head. Actually, she couldn't give an answer to the doctor. She had not even tried to explain the reasons for her presence. She was upset and offended. So she merely made a gesture of acquiescence, turned her back, and went away, ashamed and confused.

CHAPTER 4
THE GIRL

At twenty-four years old, Joyce Gallagher was a happy and truthfully pretty young lady. At this age, she still hadn't a boyfriend, an unusual thing for a young girl having past already six years in a university. It wasn't that because boys didn't like her. On the contrary, since her fourteen years, teenagers were chasing after her. And on campus, she was the most coveted Southern aristocratic star. She was the only girl from a wealthy agro industrial, from the city of Arabe, little municipality of Alabama, a place where there was no susceptibility problems and racial tension. Indeed, aware of this year 1992, Arabe was part of these localities of the Southern United States where the population was composed of 99.5 percent of European origin. The remaining 0.5 percent was Blacks, Asians, and natives of America. Not more than 250 people on about six thousand composed the population.

When she was born, Joyce was the center of all the attention of her family and of her city because her father, John Gallagher, was the richest, most well-known, and the one who decided to elect all the city's authorities. All residents, in one way or another, owed him something. This influence was also found in political, religious, and aristocratic circles of Montgomery, where he had most of his business.

The Gallaghers were part of a very long tradition of White conservatives, originally from Ireland who had made their fortune first in the slave trade, the workforce, agricultural production, and then the processing of food products. Political influences had enabled them, after the end of slavery, to benefit from the forced labor dare jailers of penitentiaries nearby the area or cheap labor because they fixed the cost of work and penalties against those that did not give them satisfaction. From father to son, the parents of her mother controlled the largest prison in the region and were locked up in a penitentiary population in 80 percent of Blacks and 15 percent of Hispanics and other ethnic components. The remaining 5 percent were Whites sentenced for violence against women, rapes, and a few racist murders. Offenses committed on Whites by non-Whites were rare. The judges from all the surrounding areas were not stinted to send in houses or factories controlled by the Gallaghers for any wrongdoing, the inmates chained and non-Whites who worked twelve hours a day. In return, their positions were provided to life, and they were handsomely rewarded. That deal was a quid of the alliance that worked perfectly well including during elections. Everyone voted Republican including non-Whites.

When Joyce was born, her father was so disappointed that he wanted a boy to perpetuate the family tradition. His careless behavior had not escaped Mary, his wife, which made him a countenance at the hospital in front of some hospital personnel. He apologized openly, bought her flowers to impress the witnesses, and forgot that entire thing the day after. But at home, he kept a coldness disconcerting toward the child and her mother. Two years later, she made a miscarriage of a boy of five months. It would take the intervention of his pastor to support him. Then the scenario was repeated twice in less than two years. Finally, the doctor advised his wife to no longer try to get pregnant; his life depended on it. For a conservative, misogynist, antiabortion, and against any contraceptive method, it was the worst curse. At the age of thirty-two, he decided to limit sexual relations to a minimum and acquiesce himself to accept that a girl might as well carry on family traditions. Thus, he turned all his affections to Joyce who subsequently became the largest competitor of her mother.

Joyce had a princess childhood. Instead of her mother, she was everywhere with her father. He did everything to make her known as being the one who was the closest to him and that whoever wanted a favor from the father had to lionize his princess. In the end, everybody agreed that she was really friendly, extraordinary, and devoid of discrimination. Everyone loved her even if they hated her father and disregard her mother for his aggressive character, especially for little people. Workers, maids, businessmen, politicians, religious people of the church, and even these little people that her mother discriminated were granted special attention. She was sunshine.

The eighty-first years of her life were a wonderful tale of a princess. They were passed in innocence and sexual abstinence. During her free time, she was always in business with her father, and for this one, no boy was good enough for her, even though he already sensed what part, in a pinch, he could accept only when Joyce would have finished her academic studies.

To the end of high school, Joyce was naturally admitted at the Alabama University, an old institution that profited donations every year from her father. He had insisted that she choose the business administration. It was not her first choice. She had to admit that a member of the family had to be prepared to take over the family business that her father would not have wished a cousin or a stranger put his hand in it and destroy all that of the generations had built, especially at a time when he was beginning to have eyebrows of money. Chinese competition had made lower profits, and the bank had already refused the credits he needed to modernize its facilities and become competitive.

Joyce was not only pretty and well educated but also smart and full of imaginations. She was not like these rich Republican conservative girls who were preparing to make their lives behind that of their husbands and for whom studying was unnecessary. On this side, her father agreed with her. She was the opposite of her mother, a traditional southern housewife without responsibility and without personal opinion other than that of her husband or the traditional oligarchy of Arabe. So she worked a lot and stood aloof from the easy pleasures of the campus. For her classmates and friends, she was considered as boring. Every time the opportunity was presented, she went to her father's office to work as a simple employee respecting her supervisor's requirements. This was what, moreover, made her reputation and earned her the respect and admiration of all.

At the age of twenty-five, she was about to finish her master's degree in business administration. She was preparing to spend two years studying finance despite the pleas of her father who hoped to see her start working for real. She thought she was too young and always in lack of experiences for the responsibilities that he wished to entrust her. She was a strong personality, the only one who could stand up to her father. That was, in particular, the line of character that had impressed her father to the point that he did not take any decision without referring to her. She had new ideas and a better knowledge of modernity than any other member of the family. Therefore, the opening toward the world outside Montgomery was intrigued by and totally unknown for her. She wanted also to enjoy the world, out of the closed trails in the south in order to better understand the outside world. At this time, Arabe was a rural town and sometimes frankly peasant. It was like New York, Chicago, Los Angeles, San Francisco, or Miami was in another country or another continent.

That day when Joyce hit Ray, her horizon was disturbing. It was for the first time that she found herself sticking to a man, especially in such an embarrassing position. She didn't imagine before that a colored man could be as rigid toward her and especially without any prejudice. She had studied the recent history of the south with her struggles for civil rights, but in reality, she never had direct contact with educated Black people. She assumed that Ray wasn't an Afro-American, for there was in his regard and especially in his accent. But she couldn't get any idea of this man because she never had contact with other Black people at the Alabama University outside Afro-Americans. In fact, no one in her whole life, even her opponents on campus, ever treated her that way. She was the star and center of interest of all her schools, the university, the workplaces of her father, at her hometown, and this in all social settings. Everyone loved her and even adored her. Her good upbringing and her kindliness showed the best in her family and even made forgotten the past slavery of her parents and grandparents and especially their links with the Ku Klux Klan.

Joyce had a silhouette that made her look like a Barbie doll. She had lightness in the approach and an almost angelic look. That, more than anything, had always charmed those who knew her; it was her smile and her politeness. Normally, in this part of the south, young girls of this caliber were pretentious and arrogant. It was just the opposite. She always had the same Black nanny since her birth. It was through her that she had a true maternal link. Their relationship had always shocked those who weren't family. But she had the temper of those people who didn't care what others said. She was enjoying the attention that all house employees loved her and that, without doubt, raised her curiosity about racial issues. Without knowing it, this human feeling would capsize her heart and help her cope with the most crucial moments of youth.

CHAPTER 5
THE DUDE

R ay Gaillard was, because of his origin and his education, the opposite of Joyce. His family was of Haitian origin from a small town located normally at about three hours and twenty-five minutes from the capital by paved road. As the road was dirty, in rainy weather, if they were lucky, it took more than six hours to do the 172 kilometers linking Saint-Michel-de-l'Attalaye to Port-au-Prince. It was a hassle.

The Gaillards were a family of the small province, liberal, and frankly traditionalist middle class. It was a common situation in the part of the country where local whiskey was like holy water and sex was the last meal of the day for adults only. With the arrival of the entrepreneur Louis Dejoie, who implanted in the fifties a vetiver and lemongrass industry, the city had reached meteoric economic progress that attracted a significant internal migration, including descendants from Europe and the Middle East.

The Gaillard family was part of a higher traditional caste that occupied the highest functions of the city from years: judge, mayor, school principal, city hall clerk, public health officer, etc. It was also an ancestry of large landowners that benefited from the generosity of the different governments and did not pay taxes, of course. When Jonathan Gaillard, Ray's father, was fifteen years old, he was sent to Port-au-Prince to continue his high school that he finished brilliantly. Then with the connections of his family in the new government, he obtained a scholarship for Belgium where he studied agro industry. Back home in 1953, he was engaged in the factories of Louis Dejoie II, a very important position. Five years later, he married Marie Louise Bellefleur, a teacher at the Sisters of Saint Joseph of Cluny School, a very privileged institution at the time.

But things were already going wrong as soon as the new president was sworn on October 22, 1957. François Duvalier, the new election on September 22 at the same year, began the hunting of former supporters of Louis Dejoie to the point of shutting down his factory which was the lung of the city. This year, his eldest daughter had just been born while Jonathan Gaillard had just lost his job. Knowing that this was a short-term situation, he spent his time to cultivate tobacco on the grounds of his parents while remaining outside of any political activity. Knowing that he was the head of the campaign by Louis Dejoie at Saint Michel during the elections, the private militia of Duvalier, without any reason, accused him to sustain contact with the opponent's armed network, the famous Camoquins, who was preparing a new armed insurrection to overthrow the government.

In the evening of September 22, 1960, Jonathan Gaillard received a telegram from a friend of the government intelligence department with whom he had studied in Belgium. He enjoined him to leave town immediately because as part of a new purge, the order was given to arrest him with his whole family and led to the Fort Dimanche in Port-au-Prince, the detention center of political prisoners. He knew that few would come back alive in this prison. Late at night, as the city slept—before the militia of city of Gonaïves came to take him away, as was the case for many families across the country—Jonathan Gaillard loaded two horses, took a few things, and fled to Dondon. From there, he headed toward Ouanaminthe from where he crossed the border to take refuge in the Dominican Republic.

When the Tontons Macoute, the personal army of President Duvalier, arrived in Saint Michel late at night, the Gaillards were already far away in the mountains. The gunmen questioned the two servants in vain. They did not know anything about their employer's plans. Caught in rage, they killed them before setting the house on fire. That night, they searched the whole city, even going to wake up the whole neighborhood to interview people one by one. Was it not the courage of the mayors, the judge of peace, and the police chief, they would have executed all the neighbors of the Gaillards before leaving? Eight days later, his friends sold his possessions and sent him the money that he used to pay for visas for the whole family. When he arrived at Miami, he settled to Fort Lauderdale with friends he had known when he was working in the factories in his hometown. Two weeks later, he rented a small two-room apartment comfortable enough for its little income. Mrs. and Ms. Gaillard took English courses at evenings and worked day shift with fake papers, one as a security guard and the other as a nanny in an affluent couple.

Six months after they arrived in Miami, the Gaillards obtained legal papers, thanks to the intervention of a network of former supporters of Louis Dejoie who paid lawyers to get the status of political exiles. Since then, they had quickly integrated because of their high level of education and the name of Gaillard who revealed their Louisiana origin. Links had even been established with other families in this southern state of the United States. As soon as their capabilities to express themselves correctly in English were established, they changed status quickly. Marie Louise Gaillard was appointed as a substitute teacher in an elementary school, and her husband worked as a technician on a large plantation producing oranges and lemons. Subsequently, his boss braced the chance he had to have been able to get hold of a well-trained expert. To encourage him to remain faithful, given the lack of qualified resources in this area, he facilitated the purchase of a charming house in the region of West Palm Beach and a new car.

It's a happy family who saw what happened in 1962—the son she was expecting so much. Ray Gaillard was born on August in West Palm Hospital, very healthy, and with a smile that announced its success with women. In the neighborhood where he grew up, being the youngest child, he had become the center of attention because of his kindness. The fact that his family was the only Black in this area was not a concern. Instead, his father and his mother became friends with the families of other children that they invited, at every opportunity, to come to enjoy Haitian exotic foods. Thus, he grew in an environment free of all complex and any discrimination. The Gaillards were so well integrated into American society that they adopted American nationality despite Haitian nationalist reflexes of departure. So when Ray decided at the end of his sociology studies at Miami University to join the United States Navy, his parents did not hesitate to give him his blessing.

The ordinary life they were living made the Gaillards as an ordinary American family and without history like all the others in this district of West Palm Beach. What they were trying to make clear to everyone was the time when Ray was disrespected by supremacists Whites in a club of Miami. That day, he was on leave and visiting his parents. He was having good time with a group of childhood friends when he was approached by three young White men. They were already intoxicated and under the influence of drugs. They had started with the insult before they disrespected him with racist talk. One of them jostled him and even tried to pour him a bottle of beer on his head. But in spite of the many provocations, not only had he avoided the brawl, but also he had equally calmed down his White friends who wanted to react. Then he left the club without making any comments and went home to spend the night at his house. His behavior and composure had impressed the owner that had informed of his status as a sub-officer and son of immigrants. The next day, he called the television news that made a biopic about Ray, his family, his childhood, and his presence in the marines. Even his commander and his uniformed comrades took advantage of the events. He had become the celebrity of his unit. Two weeks later, he was introduced by his commander to two recruiter officers who, having been informed of its history, wanted to evaluate his capabilities in order to propose its integration in the Navy Seal, the Army's elite.

Ray integrated the Navy Seal after his assessment and his training which placed at the highest level of the new graduates. He was involved in many clandestine operations. Then during a mission, he was seriously wounded in saving the lives of many of his comrades and while allowing his unit to reach his objective. He spent ten days in a coma and three months in intensive care. After the rehabilitation process in a special army center, he was sent back to civilian life with large compensations.

He received the medal of Congress and several decorations, both the president and the army.

Two years after his disengagement, Ray was contacted by the Drug Enforcement Administration (DEA) for infiltrating Haitian Army, Government, and other sectors who involved in drug trafficking and money laundering. His military past and American hero earned him a great reputation in its origin country. It was a major asset. So when he arrived in Port-au-Prince, all doors were opened to him, including in the business community that laundered the money. He attended the associations of the students, the business, and politic organizations with his patriotic discourse and sociological background. He gave many conferences in universities and the military academy while publishing articles in the oldest newspaper in the country. In a very short time, Ray had become a popular figure around the country.

When Jean Bertrand Aristide ran for office in October 1991, he supported him and advised those responsible for his personal security. On February 7, 1992, he became officially his closest military adviser while continuing to collaborate with the various army units including the command center. His position allowed him to collect easily information on drug trafficking and money laundering process linking Haiti, Colombia, Jamaica, Dominican Republic, Panama, United States, and the Caribbean countries also serving as a front door for the European Union. As soon as his arrival in Port-au-Prince on September 30, 1992, he oversaw a network of information that was never set up by the DEA in Haiti. For the first time since his release from the university, he lived a life filled with good surprises. He had a beautiful girlfriend, a luxury apartment paid by the DEA, a nice car, and enough money to live the lifestyle of a prince.

CHAPTER 6
THE UNPREDICTABILITY OF FATE

The accident that brought Ray at the hospital had a significant impact on Joyce and the University of Alabama. The dean offered him immediately after the events an agreement to avoid a lawsuit and especially bad publicity. Ray had accepted it without any discussion since he had no intention of making a history of it. When his convalescent period ended, he was accepted to the programs eagerly. His military past and his event had made his reputation and some bad jokes for Joyce. To tell the truth, the girls were chasing him as soon as he arrived. He was one that everyone wanted to be friends on the campus.

One year since Ray returned to the United States of America, he was still getting lost. The trauma he had experienced in the Navy Seal began again after his Haitian misadventures. However, he had become rich. Brian, his financial agent, informed him that his investments flourished and the future was still more enchanting. He advised him to spend a low life to not let people think about his real financial situation. He didn't buy a car as he could not accept to have a cheap one. So he lived alone like any other student, a normal life. At thirty-two years old, he already had a long past behind him. In spite of many solicitations from the prettiest young girls, he did not formally have a girlfriend. He was dating some girls for sex and for having company in a town where he was just beginning to know. He was still haunted by the tragic death of his fiancée in Haiti, especially as Col. Fred Joseph Altieri had informed him that Sarah's body had never been found in spite of his many efforts. He still felt guilty for not having saved her. The psychologist in the service of veterans had brought, of course, a valuable help, but this could not completely compensate for the painful memories that continued to haunt him. He could not erase from his mind the last image of disfigured Sarah's dead body that he had seen and the fact that the woman he should get married was buried in a common pit. The only memories he kept from his relationship were the engagement ring that he carried in his finger and a picture of her that he preserved in his purse. He did enlarge it in black and white for a large portrait on the wall in his office at home.

Ray and Joyce led a separate life. They did their best to not meet, although they had common friends. The only time they were face-to-face was in a meeting held on the campus by students who were promoting nondiscrimination and nonviolence. They looked at each other in the eyes, greeted with courteous gestures, and turned their backs. She had wanted to talk to him. Besides, his heart throbbed harder when their eyes met, but the pretty girl who was beside Ray gave the impression of being more than just a friend. So she pretended falsely to give little interest to this man who too seemed to be doing the same thing when their eyes were linking.

Joyce was doing her best to never talk about Ray with her friends. She avoided any conversation about him or was slipping away every time somebody named him in its presence. But in the truth, she had never stopped thinking of him. It had become an obsession as long as he occupied her thought. However, she knew the unfriendliness that separated them. Moreover, despite the severity of the accident she had with Ray, her father had made a few cases. His only concern was that this son of a bitch did not have any lawsuit against his daughter. When he was certain that it would not happen, he diverted the conversation whenever his daughter tried to get his impressions. All he wanted was that journalists don't ask a question and that the NACCP doesn't look around his private life. It would have been even more damaging to his affairs which continued to deteriorate.

Everyone seemed to turn their backs on this misfortune when there was another incident that was going to change the lives of the Gallaghers forever.

This Tuesday morning, like all the others since the beginning of this semester, Joyce left her home at 7:00 a.m. to get to her class that began one hour later. She was really upset and, for the first time, in anger against her father. When she started her car, he didn't come to kiss her as he usually did. In the evening, they had a vigorous talk. Indeed, John Gallagher, her father, had an ally at her mother to compel her to agree to go out with Roy Wilkens, the son of the best friend in the family, the police chief of Arab. This was not the first time this conversation was coming back during dinner. But every time, Joyce was contented to dodge it on the pretext that she had given priority to her studies. She knew that the young man's mother was pressing her own to intervene since he was too intimidating to open his heart to her. This marriage would save John Gallagher's financial problems. But she had clearly left to understand her parents that she was not for sale and that the first man in her life would be the one she had chosen herself. She had left the dinner to rush into her room with tears in her eyes. She never thought that her parents could get there.

In this Tuesday also, Ray left his home to go to college, as he usually did since its complete rehabilitation. He had hung his backpack and proposed to walk the blocks of the street that separated the auditorium. By the same way, the people of the neighborhood had eventually developed an almost personal relationship with him. He had finally given them his name on various occasions, but some women continued to call him courteously the handsome young Black man. There were even some ladies who looked at him as a sex symbol that they were ready to cheat on their partners only to spend a good time with him. He had finally established intimate relationships with everyone, starting with the grocer, hairdresser, managers of small restaurants, ladies retired who were jogging, or teenagers playing tuff guy, etc. The light rain was just stopped, and the road was plenty wet. Ray crossed the intersection of the third block when a vehicle, ignoring the stop signaling, crossed the crossroads in turn. The young woman behind the wheel was driving at sixty miles an hour with vision obscured by tears that flowed in her eyes and the windows of the car filled with vapor. She had not paid attention to the road signs or to the pedestrian crossing the street. She struck Ray with a full whip and pushed him to three meters from the vehicle. In fact, the young woman had time to brake only after the impact. So the vehicle slipped on the pavement with a crash before hitting two others in the park. The airbag was blown off and hit her face. Fortunately, she only had some fear. She hadn't had any trauma. But when she raised her head, she noticed that the glass of his vehicle was broken. What worried her still were those people that rushed to help a man that was spread over the plants on the other side. Before she had time to move, volunteers had come to pull her out of her vehicle. Three minutes later, the police arrived in the area with two ambulances.

Nobody told her about the identity of the victim or his real health condition. They merely told her that he had lost consciousness. When she arrived at the hospital, she was sent to the emergency room, and a nurse reassured her that the accident victim wasn't dead. The doctor merely checked that she hadn't had any trauma before sending her back home. Her father came to pick her up as soon as he had been informed by the police. Once back home, she hurried on her bed, comforted by her mother and Alison, her former nanny.

Later on in the afternoon, two police officers went to her home to interrogate her on the morning incident because they had learned that this was the second time that Ray was received in the hospital for an accident caused by her. At the sight of the police car, he had a wind of panic at the house. But it was soon dissipated when they explained the reasons for their visit. At this time, Joyce learned the name of the victim. She couldn't hold herself; she uttered a cry and collapsed. Even her father was surprised by the coincidence.

As usual, Mary Gallagher felt pain in silence. Her horizon was never her daughter who had stolen the attention and affection of her husband. She had, indeed, rushed to her daughter, but it was one police who laid her on the sofa, and it was Alison who made her come back. In fact, that day, she was fortuitously in Montgomery. While Joyce's mother sat beside her, Alison went to the kitchen to make her a cup of tea. The police officers were proposed to come back again another time if necessary, providing that she shouldn't have anything to investigate, the young lady hadn't had any idea of the victim's identity at the time of the accident. They also assumed that she wasn't driving under any influence of drugs or alcohol.

Ray awoke in the hospital eight hours later with a plaster foot, a bandage on his head, and tubes everywhere. During his unconscious time, he had a lot of medical tests and x-rays. According to the hospital, it was really lucky.

Ray did not know the author of the accident either. Moreover, no one had come to speak to him even after he had regained consciousness. For the time being, the doctor advised him to rest for twenty-four hours before receiving a visit. He could go out in four days. The next day, his parents—including his big sister, his brother-in-law, and their twins of two years—arrived from Florida and were alerted by the city police who had their phone number by the university. His father and his mother lived at his home while his sister, her husband, and her sons went to the hotel.

The same police officers, who had surrendered at Joyce before, met Ray at the hospital. They wanted to question him about the accident in order to complete their report. Before answering the police questions, Ray asked them with a smile that reassured them to tell him the name of the elephant that had overthrown him. The policemen burst out laughing. It was too funny. The noise alerted nurses and doctors, by an unaccustomed situation in a hospital. With unusual humor for a policeman, he explained to him that was the same elephant that had already hit him at the university a few months previously. Ray was astonished at the news. The coincidence was a surprise for everybody. It was like winning a lottery twice with the same number. Everyone was sadly surprised by the coincidence. They were making fun and premonitory about it. The hospital room of Ray became a real forum of experts on marital issues. They all predicted that this girl was predestined for him and that they were doing a couple bound by an explosive relationship. The time seemed to stop in this room, and for a moment, the accident appeared to be a good thing and a sign of destiny.

While jokes were well underway, no one seemed to notice this figure standing in the doorway for more than ten minutes. She had heard it all.

In Ray's room, everyone seemed to take pleasure in something that was the biggest disaster of her life. Soundless, she followed the situation with enchantment when Jonathan and Marie Louise Gaillard touched her shoulders. She jumped and apologized nicely. Ray immediately noticed the silhouettes of his parents and made them a gesture of the hand, which returned the others to the door. The face of Joyce appeared as a ghost. It was an embarrassing silence.

Ray's father and mother did not appear, having failed to make what was going on before. It was in this suspicious silence that settled in the room that Jonathan and his wife said to everybody an expressive hello and asking if it was Jay Leno's show. To break the sudden silence definitely, one policeman turned to Ray to tell him by gesturing and with a full smile, "Sir, I present your elephant." It was a moment of real sympathy.

That second time between Ray and Joyce was very much better. They became acquainted and started laughing at their bad luck. She also became acquainted with his parents who even began to talk to her about their country. The presence of the Gaillards helped to relax the atmosphere especially since the girl was really charming.

Joyce had taken the time to be prepared before to come to the hospital. She didn't say a word to her parents after Alison convinced her to go there. They thought that she had to spend the day at the university. But after the economic class she followed with little interest, she took the road to the hospital without really knowing how she's going to have access to Ray's room and especially how to approach it. Fortunately, everyone in the nurse's station was in Ray's room. This had facilitated her intrusion. Now that things had happened for the best, she didn't want to leave. For more than three hours, she kept talking with Ray and his parents about everything. And it seemed like she switched with that family. Still Ray stayed on guard. He had some friends at the university that informed him about the past of the Gallaghers and the situation in Arab city where these people had their roots for over two hundred years.

When the Gaillards decided to go back home to have some rest, it was Joyce who proposed to bring them back in spite of protests from Jonathan. Before leaving the room, she gave Ray a beautiful smile that already said a lot about what she had on her heart. Then she guaranteed to return the next day with news of the university. She proposed herself to go see the dean so that he would not penalized Ray for his absences.

On the way to Ray's home, Joyce and the Gaillards kept talking. The girl needed to open up and clear her mind of the stress she had accumulated during her last days. She also wanted to learn from this cool family whose son had occupied her mind for several months. At last, when they arrived, Marie Louise invited her to come for a coffee. She didn't hesitate. It looked like she even wanted to invite herself during the ride. When she got into the apartment, she discovered an exotic world as she had never seen before. It was a world full of culture, Afro-Haitian made of paintings, modern and contemporary arts, fashioned metal, stones, etc. The house was reminiscent of life of culture and happiness. The interior showed the cultural richness of Ray's country of origin. In his office, she discovered the great black-and-white picture of Sarah. The pulpy and sexy face of the picture showed off a young lady with sensuality that she'd never seen before. That got her an idea of Ray's life. Marie Louise saw her remained silent in front of the portrait. She had been killed tragically, she told her! But you should never talk to Ray about her.

Joyce spent a good time with the Gaillards. She became acquainted with Ray's sister, her husband, and her sons who came for dinner at the house. Unsurprisingly, they invited the girl to join them. It was a unique experience for her. She opened her natural curiosity instantly to enjoy the foods that were unknown so far, and she was delighted. She spent a good time before leaving, lost in his family traditional references. The stereotypes of American traditional southern family flew into pieces that day. She realized that society in which she had evolved had taught her prejudices and unfounded complexes and especially away from reality. Once home, she spoke to her mother about the visit at the hospital and how she met with the Gaillards by accident. She wanted to know where she spent her day since she returned home to an advanced hour of the night. She didn't want to lie. It was not in her habits. By listening to her, her mother immediately got it. Her daughter was in love with a Black person, an immigrant, and a Haitian. That was a combination of factors in a single man that would make her father frenzy more than anything else. She displayed a sarcastic laugh that her daughter quickly understood. As a conservative mother who lived in the Deep South of the

United States, she took time to prevent her against the family rules. After vain protests, Joyce had finally accepted that she had some feelings, but it was nothing other than sympathy caused by the discovery of a world previously unknown to her. But Mary Gallagher wasn't born yesterday. She knew that if her daughter had been able to get there, this feeling should be something true and strong. Although Roy Wilkens Junior was her favorite, she did nothing out of her disappointment. She did not want to fight against a woman in love, especially when it came to the first one. Joyce had already been twenty-five years old; she could decide to turn her back on the family to indulge in her passions. It was a perspective that Mary didn't want to consider for now. Despite everything, she loved her daughter, and she just wanted her happiness.

The Gaillards were not fooled either. They had detected also this small light shining in Joyce's eyes. This reminded them of their own history. As Haitian families never talk about the romantic life with the children, they did not blow a single word to Ray.

Two days later, before resuming and going back to Florida, the Gaillards went together at the hospital for the last time. The whole family was around Ray. It was a time of friendliness that brought an unusual warmness that disturbed the other patients. The nurses had left this good mood out of standards that warmed a place habitually gloomy.

In the other rooms adjoining Ray's, patients and their relatives were at the beginning offended by the gleaming laughter. Then as the conversations grew, they paid attention with complacency especially not to be stigmatized as a racist in this part of the hospital that received the only black patient.

Joyce arrived at the time when the Gaillards was leaving the hospital to the airport. She had never seen goodbyes as happy like this one. She was pretty embarrassed. She thought that these people were going to believe she was running after their son. But at the truth, she wondered herself why she was there, if otherwise, to catch Ray's attention! Then she did not care about what people were thinking. What could she do! She had lived this long night only to return to the hospital. It was stronger than her. Realizing that her presence was desired, she even proposed to drive the Gaillards to the airport. But they refused in a concert of voices who said a lot about their state of mind. Joyce got the point at the same time as Ray. "My daughter," said Marie Louise Gaillard while she gave a mother kiss to the young lady, "preferably take care of him. I know, like his father, how he can act like a big baby." Then she turned her back after kissing Ray once again before she left the room.

Hugs and small words whispered by the fellow stuck the head of Joyce as a heavyweight to bear. She was not expecting as much sign of sympathy on people she didn't know yet seventy-two hours ago. It looked like they were pushing her into Ray's arms.

Once the Gaillards left, an incredible silence filled the room. Joyce did not know how to start with, and she could not really justify the reason for this new visit. Doctor's arrival broke the inconvenience. He brought good news. Indeed, he informed Ray that he could leave as soon as the next day. As the matter of fact, the medical exams did not reveal any complication. He would, however, return to the hospital every two weeks for follow-up and evaluation during the next three months until the plaster he wore at the foot had been removed. Joyce stood quietly near the entrance door while the doctor spoke to Ray. But from time to time, he looked behind to admire the young lady. A beautiful person like her never go ignored. Her presence in the room of a Black man in a hospital in this city spontaneously raised questions.

The doctor went away finally. This was the first time that Ray and Joyce were really in the obligation to speak after the embarrassment moment. She apologized for the accident and told him with a faint smile that would be their last. Then she complimented him for his apartment and was curious about the quality of his art collection. Ray could not believe that his parents had brought her home. Eventually, the masks fell, and the conversation turned on personal banalities: their lives, Ray's military past, and his country of origin. As Haitians like to brag about their history and their culture, Joyce had had a course of history and literature for two hours. The young woman was delighted to learn that beyond her home state Alabama, its small city Arab, and the United States, that there was a wonderful world to explore. Three hours had passed without them realizing it. Then the nurse intervened to recall Joyce that the time of the visits was done for a long time and that unless she arranged to spend the night at the hospital. She begged that could happen or she could take the risk. But she couldn't explain this behavior to Ray and her family. Before turning her back definitively, she promised Ray to come tomorrow to bring him back home. Then she gave him instinctively a kiss on the forehead. While she went through the door, she blew him a last kiss of the hand. This was a girl who seemed to have wings that skirted the hospital corridor. Once in the parking lot, she didn't start the car immediately. She let herself get carried away by dreams that crossed her mind. She had never felt in this happiness before. It's like she couldn't think like a rational person she used to be at least one week ago. When finally she took the road to go back home, she opened the radio to listen to music. She fell on Franck Sinatra with his crooner voice who sang "My Way." She smiled slowly allowing the sweetness of the melody while she drove slowly into the night, the heart in the stars.

CHAPTER 7
A Romance in Small Clouds

One hour before the scheduled time for Ray's release from the hospital, Joyce was already there. It looked like she spent that night only to see him the next morning. If her father hadn't noticed this light which shone in her eyes, her mother, instead, saw only the beginning of something that would disturb the peace of the family. Financial difficulties had hidden the reflex to her husband and had done away with family concerns. It's like he lost that incredible charm that kept their love alive. Worse was he couldn't see the changes that were operated in the life of his daughter who was his little princess. Now he spent his time between his factory trying to save it from bankruptcy and his apartment in Montgomery. He was rarely home in Arab and for very short periods. The family couldn't be together only from time to time to Montgomery when he gave him a break. Even Joyce who lived with him in the same apartment in Montgomery could not see him. They were rarely together at the same time even on Sunday. Without him, life at Arab wasn't the same like when the family lived happy hours with plenty of Black servants, flatterers who came to party, and politicians who required favors.

On leaving the house, Joyce was really superb in this simple dress but too sexy for just to go for a McDonald. That's what, more than anything else, worried her mother. When she arrived at the hospital, everybody looked at her. It was really a good dream to see someone like that. She was the beauty, the stylishness, the grace, and the litheness combined in a single body in appearance completely uncompleted. Joyce walked to Ray's room, awake of the effect she was making on others. She left floppy behind her, the stunning looks, a gracious, and quite drunken perfume.

Joyce went through the front door of Ray's room with a light step and a surreptitious look. She looked suspicious believing that she could meet someone else in the room. Fortunately, there was nobody. Ray had already on a dress, asleep on the bed with earphones in the ear. Mozart's music made him look calm and frankly childish. The girl was on the charm. She took a seat next to the bed and looked at him passionately. It looked like she wanted to join him just to lay her head deeply on his arms and get into his dreams. Even the sudden appearance of the nurse, her fascination would have lasted a long time. The nurse looked at the girl blushing. She smiled at her courteously. They were the same age, and having already gone through it, she understood this state of mind. The love eyes were not cheating. They exchanged an accomplice look and smiled before getting "hi" at the same time. But Joyce protested without persuasion when the nurse tried to talk about her boyfriend. It was the sound of their voice that woke up Ray. He stretched to chase the stiffening from an unfinished sleep and rose to sign the papers. He asked them jokingly if they were talking about him while bending his head to look at them from the corner of the eyes. "Oh no," they repeated in one way. Then they laughed together of a harmony that resounded a fragrance of youthfulness in a world of carefree and beauty.

Ray seized his staves and stood a line toward the door. This was not the first time that he was using it, so it wasn't the end of the world. And then in the presence of ladies, he had to play the strong one. In the hallway of the hospital, it's a parade of uninterrupted and questioning looks that led to the exit. It was like an action movie when the spectators applauded the hero who went in the direction of the sunset with the girl clinging to him behind his bike.

Joyce and Ray didn't speak during the ride. They simply exchanged some glances, sneaky smiles, and onomatopoeia. Something in each of them was burning inside as an unknown desire. There was tenderness of the car, they didn't know how to start with. In any case, they knew, without saying, that a page had just turned and that they would have to find the way to start their new relationship. When the car stopped in front of the house, Ray came down and turned his back without inviting her. But she went down, passed him quite naturally, drew a key from her bag, and opened the door. Ray looked at her, all surprised by her incredible audacity. He imagined that his mother had given her this key, knowing that she was his girlfriend or that she wanted to give a boost to unlock the situation. But as an ex-soldier, he should give the impression of having mastery of the situation. But when he walked through the kitchen, he felt simply amazing. He noticed that the table was served. Paradoxically, it was Joyce who invited him to eat. In fact, since her meeting with her parents, the young girl kept taking initiatives and pushing him to overcome his shyness.

It was Saturday, the weather was splendid. It was like one of those splendor spring days that get better at the sunset and the flowers burst the petals dedicated to love and kindness. Joyce and Ray looked out the window, seeing the activities of the street, trying to swallow the Chinese foods purchased by Joyce two hours ago. It was the magic of their feet touching under the table that put them on. But they couldn't really tell who had taken the initiative first as long as the attraction was in unconsciousness. One hour later, at the end of their feelings, Ray was surprised to find that the most beautiful girl in the town of Arab and Alabama University was a virgin. Joyce remained in Ray's arms as if she had found the sacrament of the youth she was expecting at her eighteen years. Until she was completely satisfied, five hours later, she decided to get back home.

Since that memorable day, Ray and Joyce maintained a strong, passionate, and discreet relationship. Every morning, she picked him up to go to university and came back together to study or to have a good time. They were always together and their story became the romance of the whole campus. It was by a phone call from the dean of the university that John Gallagher learned about the romance.

Some White students of the university didn't appreciate that a Black man was dating the most beautiful girl on campus. So not happy to circulate racist and threatening brochures about Ray, they had tagged

Joyce's car of insults and swastikas. To avoid something worst, the dean called the police but also asked John to talk to his daughter because he didn't want to make waves because Ray also was a perfect student and a national hero, as Ray had also kept a low profile by avoiding to inform the press and the NACCP after those racist events despite the insistence of some friends. The next day, John hired a private detective in order to collect the maximum information on Ray and his romance with his daughter.

At the end of the university session, Joyce flew to Haiti against her father's advice. She claimed that it was a study-and-research trip as part of the preparation for her PhD. But John Gallagher wasn't fooled. The Haitian military who had wanted to kill him was no longer in power. Ray and his girlfriend visited the country without any fear, especially since he was sheltered by some American soldiers as part of the United Nations Mission that had landed in Haiti on October 1994 to reinstate President Aristide to the power. He took advantage to visit Sarah Altieri's brother who was appointed general on the official recommendation of the State Department. He visited his old friends and did sing a mass in Sacre-Coeur-de-Turgeau Church in memory of his missing fiancée.

This was Joyce's first trip outside the United States. After two weeks visiting Haiti, Ray and his girlfriend spent time at West Palm Beach with his parents and crossed New Orleans, Chicago, by rental car before making a detour by New York. They came back to Montgomery by plane at the end of August, happy and joyful. That day, Joyce lost her handbag at the airport with all personal stuff including her passport and her diary. In the same evening, her father almost had a cardiac arrest by reading what the detective certified that he hadn't been aware of it. But John Gallagher didn't say anything to his wife. He drank whiskey for the first time to forget his shamefulness and slept at his office at night. He didn't want to see the face of his daughter. When he woke up early in the morning, he made himself a black coffee and took his time to think about how to destroy this Negro who did his best to destroy his reputation as much as in his hometown.

CHAPTER 8
THE BROKEN DREAM

The American people didn't take a joke with some of their traditions, as their barbecue for Fourth of July, the Super Bowl, and Thanksgiving among others. They were blessed. The July 4 barbecue had its importance, but fever raised the Super Bowl, and the Thanksgiving was unparalleled in American culture. It's a way of living that grew as a tradition fundamentally and exclusively national better than baseball or basketball with its practices to profess a religion.

In the Deep South, being White was a privilege. It was like practices and traditions that people don't joke particularly in small cities like Arab. Being White was a passport that gave access to a lot of freedoms and preserved against other ethnic groups and liberals in a community that elected their sheriff, judges, and mayors depending on criteria racial. It was with pride that the American invited a stranger home for Thanksgiving to share more than dinner with the turkey but part of their culture and all also a family tradition in some cases.

In this year, as tradition required, John Gallagher prepared to go back to Arab for Thanksgiving dinner. Joyce would like to avoid it this time, knowing that's going to be the time to talk about the thing that would upset the family: her relationship with Ray. But it was a custom to which she could not differ and which she hated since she had learned at her expense that in families like the Gallaghers, Republicans, and Nationalists, a woman had to stay pretty and quiet in political discussions, the football game in TV, and other social issues. Mentally, she was preparing to face the first big crisis of her life.

Since she was back from Haiti, John Gallagher spoke little to his daughter. He systematically avoided her. He rarely put his feet to Arab and didn't speak also once to his wife. Irritated by this careless behavior, Mary decided to stop to go to Montgomery. She stayed in Arab definitely. She had, at the beginning, a repugnance for this apartment in Montgomery, too cramped and very uncomfortable for a lady of her rank.

Since he knew about the relationship between his daughter with the son of immigrants, as he called him now, John Gallagher followed strict sexual abstinence. It seemed that the relationship between Ray and Joy made him so mad inside that he put off his frustration on his wife, symbolizing for his weakness and especially the loss of what was this part of White America. He would have had that stigma fallen on his family. If it wasn't the religious faith and fear of scandal in this small town where the adultery of the wife was worse than death, Mary Gallagher would have already cheated on her husband. Even Ray was Black, Joyce's mother felt inside an admiration of the love her daughter devoted to him. That love broke all the racial restrictions and the old-age prejudices of two White families in a small town where supremacism was still very present in the everyday life of the entire population at the end of the twentieth century.

John Gallagher did his best to hide his disappointment from his daughter. He secretly proposed to take care of this son of a bitch on a field where Ray wouldn't be able to have a witness in his favor. He was obsessed with the need to break this unnatural impulse of love that tarnished the image of his family. Thus, he asked Joyce to invite Ray to share with their family the Thanksgiving dinner, not as a boyfriend but as a simple guest.

Ray had already planned to spend the Thanksgiving with his family in Florida. It was also an American tradition that the Gaillards had adapted, taking into the good side of the customs of a country they had definitively learned to love and serve. He was upset with Joyce's request, but he still agreed against his will. When he called his mother to talk about it, she seemed not to make it, but she had this maternal pinch that did not augur something good. But his father was furious. He was a thoughtful and cultured man endowed with rational skepticism on American society. Therefore, upon his return from Montgomery, he had done his research on the Arab city and the secular traditions of this part of the United States of America. When his wife passed him the phone, he felt his heavy breathing. Then he spoke to him openly as if he wanted to make him understand the risk that he incurred without an attempt to make him the lesson. At the end of the conversation, he asked him to be careful because he felt that the Gallaghers weren't motivated by good intentions toward him. "You're a soldier," he said to him. "You should do what you thought be necessary whatever the price to be paid." Then he hung up. He immediately went to make two glasses of punch with Barbancourt rum in which he mixed it with coca, lemon, and two cubes of ice. He took his magazine and sat on the veranda with the delight of his wife with his favorite beverage. It was the pleasure of a quiet, happy, and peaceful retreat. His wife brought some Haitian food. It's a good evening that began in spite of the bad news. Thank God he still could hand up some woman needs and his wife never pulled him back as it was to regain their past sexual pleasures.

When Joyce went to pick him up in the morning, Ray was very sad and disappointed. He had slept poorly in the evening after the conversation with his parents. He was uncomfortable. Not only because he had to apologize for his behavior, what he hated, but also this dinner didn't augur anything good. He had the impression that the sky was going to fall on his head. But his girlfriend didn't see anything coming. Joyce was too in love and too happy to think of the wrong side of things. She believed that her father loved her and respected her enough to accept her choice.

Joyce parked her car in the front of Ray's apartment at 7:00 a.m. She planned to take the road later as possible so as to get to Arab just before dinner scheduled at nineteen hours to limit contact with her parents. Above all, she wanted to make her boyfriend in a good spirit with a symbolic gesture in order to overcome the anxiety there must have been before the meeting with her family. The first thing she did upon entering the house with breakfast in the morning was dragging Ray in the shower where they spent forty-five minutes. They ate in bed in the most perfect nudity. The sweetness of the hugs made them sleep for two hours. In truth, neither one nor the other had wanted to leave. The young woman wished that time didn't stop at the present moment. Nothing else was mattered.

When the couple left Montgomery, they took the I-65 then the US-82 directly to Arab. Instead of two hours and forty-six minutes to do the 246 kilometers separating the two cities, they spent more than four hours, taking advantage of the time to manage their stress. As the city approached, the atmosphere inside the car had become gloomy. To transform that sad moment, Joyce put the radio on that played, as by chance, an old hit song by Louis Armstrong: "I'll Be Glad When You're Dead." While listening to this strange rhyme, Ray had suddenly laughed. He would like to tell Joyce that this could be the welcome words of her parents!

When Joyce parked her car in front of the house shortly before 5:30 p.m., her mother was out on the stairs. She was waiting for her with an involuntary laugh. A person had to make a good impression on the visitor. Her husband hadn't absolutely played the hypocrite person for all the gold in Norfolk. If Joyce had given two kisses to her mother, Ray gently showed his right hand with the natural courtesy of an officer of the army. Moreover, in his mind, he had already made a good decision to endorse his military reflexes in order to deal with this situation. Already in his way of dressing, talking, smiling, and behaving, he had the rigid posture of a gentleman retained by protocol obligations.

Ray was very athletic with an extraordinary body and face. That day, he wore a navy blue sports jacket, blue jeans, a white shirt, and black boots that gave him a profile of a true James Bond. When he was at the height of Mary Gallagher, the gesture he made to remove his glasses was so theatrical, without wanting to amaze the curiosity of Joyce's mother. "Mr. Gaillard," she said when she shook his hand, "I wish you the welcome." Then they'd all crossed a large hall to head toward the veranda where John Gallagher was waiting for them with his pastor and his wife, the police chief and his wife, and the mayor of Arab and his wife. When they saw Ray arrived, they had stopped talking and looked surprised, and they stood to greet him. They did not expect to see a man so impressive, so beautiful, and so calm. It was very far from what the detective had described to John Gallagher in his report.

It wasn't a happy beginning but a courteous contact. John invited Ray to sit down between the police chief and the mayor. Something planned. It looked like a conspiracy to intimidate him and bring him to do as many mistakes as possible. His daughter sat in his left side but far from her boyfriend. The first few minutes were silent and frankly embarrassing. No one knew how to start a conversation. Finally, it was the police chief who broke the ice by asking him if he was Haitian as he had learned. Ray corrected with a truthful manner by telling that he was American of Haitian origin and former US Navy officer and Navy Seal. Everyone went quickly to start talking about his parents, poverty in his country of origin, and on the refugees that happened stubby sea on the beaches of Florida. He was forced to talk about everything they thought they could possibly bring down. But he didn't fall into the trap. He answered in the most courteous way as possible and with knowledge without bragging. He knew his story well. He admitted the realities not as a fatality but as a complex history combination related to the fact that Haiti was always the victim of the international retribution because of the African origin of its population and the commotion that it had caused by taking his independence by arms against the world's greatest nation of the eighteenth and nineteenth century. Then he explained in a few words the context of the war of independence and the decisions taken by European and American countries to make Haiti a failure estate in the eyes of Black American, the African continent, and the world and the importance of this independence for the security of the United States of America for the liberation of all South America in the fight against the slavery system, etc. It was enlightening, but other than Joyce, everyone else didn't care. Moreover, every time she tried to change the conversation to talk about his military past and his decorations by the Congress, the president, and on various occasions by the army, she was kindly ignored. Only Mary Gallagher didn't talk. The disastrous situation in Haiti was more of a conversation for them. Ray had understood the game well to remain calm. He endured polite and focused on his goal not to disappoint his girlfriend who seemed to have so much to lose as him if this relationship came to be broken. But she began to be panicked. The conversation was beginning awkwardly. During the time that they were talking, they had not even offered Ray a glass of water. There was not a joke or a smile. It looked like a meeting between Americans and Soviets during the Cold War. But the military, former navy, former Navy Seal, and former DEA agent held the misfortune with brio until dinner was served.

The configuration of the table where everybody sat down for dinner was the same as the one under the veranda. Joyce was once again isolated to Ray. The prayer made by the pastor was very hostile and announced a certain thunderstorm. He insisted on the forgiveness from the curse of Noah and the race of the elect. He insisted that God had created us as we are, slave or master, rich or poor, different from each other. He finished with an apology for submission and the fact that we must return to our Creator without turning away from his will and his choice. Then before they started eating, he asked everyone to make a wish at this time of Thanksgiving. It was something they had concocted in the absence of Joyce's mother to make Ray even more uncomfortable. John Gallagher should be the last to talk and the one who wished everyone bon appetit.

Mary Gallagher was kind, very simple, and very courteous. Ray had won a little grace in her eyes. Apart from his skin color, he was her kind of man.

The other women were all also polite with a tone of simplicity and Christianity that bordered the fundamentalist and total submission to marital authority. They understood that Ray was a Christian like their parents who had never been divorced and who had not committed depravities such as abortion, adultery, zoophile, etc. They, therefore, decided that God could absolve him for his other venial wickedness as the color of his skin, among others.

It's the mayor who really set the tone of what would be the rest of the evening making swear that the unity of real America was not tarnished because of grace and complacency.

Ray prayed to God that the soldiers committed on operations outside the country return safely in the next Thanksgiving and that his parents do not disinherit him to abandon them to come to Arab during this period. But that did not appease the wrath of its critics.

The police chief spoke about courage and the need for America to preserve what God had given all of them beyond humanism and the indulgence they could have for the weakest.

Joyce wanted everyone to find the good sense, love, and happiness that made the human being better. For tonight, this vow was a banality.

The wishes of John Gallagher were an unbelievable and close coldness, a little too much of the ideal White supremacist. Even before he had finished, an icy coldness crossed the table. No one had the courage to look at Ray's side. For once, they had gone too far. Mary Gallagher bowed his head, confused, and tears slowly flowed from Joyce's eyes.

John Gallagher spoke, indeed, of the need to preserve that made America great in the Deep South and how this country was built and how it could also disappear because of assimilation, weakness of a democracy imposed by a liberal fringe of society, and by an idea condescending of equality that never existed between human beings. He ended with the hope that America would one day find its greatness and its past. And with a kind of disgust expressed clearly in a marble face, he raised his glass of iced tea to wish all bon appetit.

Ray breathed a great blow, swept the table from his regard, and then stood up. He made the sign of the cross and turned to Mary Gallagher to thank her for the invitation and apologized for having to leave because he thought he wasn't really welcome. He took the direction of the door after greeting the others from the head by saying calmly, "Ladies, gentlemen." To Joyce who went to get up, he told her with a greedy smile not to give herself that trouble and he would find the way out.

When Ray crossed the frontward, the housekeepers followed him with sorrow. He didn't seem to pay any attention to them. He was so glad it was over. In this isolated street of the city, it was completely dark since there were no streetlights. A few stars twinkled in the sky as to indicate him the way to take. To tell the truth, he did not really know which direction to go. But he laughed at him madly. He had to get out of this house and this town.

A few minutes later, a police car whistled behind him. He immediately raised his hands in the air and turned slowly. The driver turned the two spotlights to better control the gestures of this stupid guy. It wasn't a place to circulate at night even at day for a non-White. The two policemen went down and robbed their weapon on Ray. Given the circumstances, he expected everything could happen, even to be targeted. As the worries ravaged him, he heard his name. One of the police officers asked the other to drop his gun. "Everything okay, Captain?" he told him. "I am sorry. You can put your hands down." Until he had found that the weapons were returned in their cases, Ray obeyed to that order. He breathed a great blow while the police came to him.

Walking slowly toward Ray, it was Roy Wilkins Junior past that came to his mind. He remembered how this man had almost died to save his life. It was his hero and his brother of color. And he was sincere! In this army unit where they both belonged, they didn't make a joke with the acquaintances. He knew that Ray kept for life the scratches of the bullets he had received for him. They were in the army special force together and had fought on several secret grounds mission together. He was his platoon officer chief, and he admired him. Roy couldn't forget that, and without thinking, he took his military posture and repeated solemnly, "Captain!" The other police officer was surprised and frozen because Roy was the son of the police chief and his father the mayor of the Arab city. Here they were, in the south of the United States of America, a Ku Klux Klan territory, facing a big Black man that the second police officer of the city greeted with deference. Fortunately, it was dark because they would have been taken for spies of NACCP. Roy offered Ray to drop him off at the station. That was all he could do for now.

Ray and Roy spoke for a few minutes in private. This gave the other officer time to call the mayor, his father. After the mayor had hung up the phone, he stood his head down and breathed slowly before telling everyone about the unexpected meeting of Ray with his son. It was like a real clap of thunder.

Joyce couldn't take it anymore. She rose from the table, looked at her father in the eyes, and left as fast as she could. But he tried in vain to dissuade her with firmness and unusual way to run after Ray. It was for the first time his wife intervened by laying her hand gently on his shoulder with unaccustomed tenderness. John Gallagher returned his head to look at her cute face and then fell silent. He grabbed a bottle of wine and poured himself a drink he lifted into the air by saying, "To the new America!" He knew, at that time, he had lost a battle. He apologized to let himself be carried away. It was Thanksgiving, and he had to do bad fortune, good heart.

When Ray left the Gallagher house, Joyce was crying. She had nearly run after him even. But her father had prevented her. Her mother was confused, shared between her husband and her daughter's broken heart.

After the toast of her father, people tried anyway to eat and watch the football game that had just begun. They had to do something else. When the phone rang, everyone was suddenly silent as if they expected news. Finally, the police chief was fixed on the concerns that worried him since Ray had left the house. He knew that he shouldn't let him go alone. In this city, people of color and other non-Whites, except for servants and workers, were never welcome. Ray was a hero, and his reputation exceeded both political parties. He was a Republican like the vast majority of officers and ex-officers. So in that circumstance, if a simple accident happened to him, that would cost them a lot. But he didn't know how to play politics with the man to whom he owed everything. He had been taken out of the blue. When he learned that Ray had been identified by a police patrol, he was really thankful. He asked the police patrol to drop him safely at the bus station and to ensure that nothing happens to him until he left the city.

Turning her back on her father with a crash, Joyce had left the house on her vehicle with a violence that made the tires squeal. She had rolled at full speed toward the bus station. Ray and Roy were there talking about the way he was going to spend the night because the first bus would leave the city only at 6:00 a.m. Roy wasn't in his good mood because he couldn't invite Ray home. At the same time, the girl arrived unexpectedly. Her car stopped with a crash beside the police car. As soon as she put her foot out, she jumped on Ray to kiss him as long she could keep her breath on. She hadn't worried about the few people who were still in this station.

Roy had a blast cut. He did not expect it. When Joyce decided to take a foot back to her boyfriend, she turned to gratify him of a friendly kiss on the cheek and a handshake to his mate. It was a shock that Roy took with philosophy.

The young deputy of the police chief looked at Joyce's vehicle and turned the corner of the street with an inside pain that he glossed over his teammate. It's the love of his life that flew away. He cursed his whole life this day of Thanksgiving. The latter patted him on the shoulder before telling him with a friendly feeling, "Anyway, love isn't forever." Then they got into the police vehicle and disappeared into the night. In a few minutes, the bus station would be temporarily closed. All Arab City watched the game and spent good time with family. He didn't have anyone in the streets.

Joyce and Ray drove to Montgomery slowly than it was, dark, and a little rain dampened the road. Throughout the trip, she had apologized at least fifteen times. They didn't speak much. They listened to music most of the time. Once downtown, they bought food from a Chinese restaurant and directed to Ray's residence. They were both very hungry. They ate and drank a few beers and slept in the early morning. It was a night with strong sensations and so far unknown. John Gallagher did not know that she had stimulated his daughter's libido to the point of making her ovulate glibly. This time, she had lost most of her rational abilities. She was caught in the torment of uncontrollable passion. From now, Ray was her charming prince, her destiny, her life, and her god.

CHAPTER 9
THE COUP

S ince the Thanksgiving night, Joyce lived at Ray's house permanently. If she informed her mother and Alison who had always been in her self-confidence at the beginning, she said nothing to her father. Anyway, he didn't want to talk to her or see her for any reason. For now, his only hope was that his daughter not become pregnant until he could find a way to end that nonsense love history.

For both lovers, there was no need to make a financial arrangement. The man had a monthly salary from the army and $100,000 he had received from the insurance company after his car accident. He never spent a dime from the investments that Brian managed with attractive gain. It wasn't necessary. Moreover, he knew that he couldn't flaunt his good fortune. But the girl was distinguished enough, also in order not to live on her concubine back. She had been in a part-time job.

In this month of April, Ray and Joyce had just completed the end-of-semester university session. Everything indicated that they were going to have good grades. The holiday season would start in a week. So they planned to go to Florida to spend some time with the Gaillards. While Ray was going shopping alone, Joyce had been lying down in the room to overcome her weakness. She didn't feel well for a few days. She could not even swallow the breakfast that Ray made especially for her before leaving. She had even vomited once but didn't say a word to Ray.

A few minutes after Ray's departure, the bell, used with determination, woke her up suddenly. It was annoying. Usually, no one visited them, and Ray never lost his keys. It was also disturbing. She wrapped a robe and rushed to the door. She just opened it when four rednecks pushed her inside. They were real tough White guys, tattooed, dressed in black, and wearing sunglasses. The only time she heard a voice was when one of them said, "We will not hurt you, but you come with us." When she woke up, she was in her room in Arab City, her mother at her side. Behind the door, she heard a voice that should be of her father who sang, "That no one else should enter this room until further notice." Now the four rednecks ensured the security of the house. All Black servants had been invited to take days off, even Alison, her only confidant. She realized that she was a prisoner of her own family. There wasn't doubt that her guardians were the members of the far White group that controlled the Arab city ever since and which her father should be the chief.

When Ray returned from his shopping, he had found the house was cleaner than he had left it. It was weird. Joyce wouldn't be able to deal with it since she felt ill. The breakfast was still on the table, and the stereo that was closed when he left was playing Louis Armstrong's song, "Bye and Bye." A feeling of emptiness showered the house. Suddenly, Ray was taken with a sense of panic. He dropped his shopping to rush to the room, but it was empty, and the bed was done. He looked into the toilet, everything was also well arranged. It was not normal. Joyce was not so neat. All personal matters from Joyce had disappeared, including her pictures. But the ones they had taken together had been cut into small pieces and left in a basket. In fact, after putting a bandana saturated in chloroform on the girl's nose, the rednecks had cleaned the house and carried away all that could suggest that she had lived there. Ray lay down on the bed to take the time to think. Then he called Joyce's number at Montgomery. The answering machine announced that it was no longer in service. This was only after that he called the police who took his statement while making the report. He had his little idea on the sudden disappearance of the girl, but he wanted to have a clean proof. One hour later, he rented a car and took the road to go to Arab city not without informing Brian before leaving.

Ray arrived at the Gallagher house at three o'clock in the afternoon. He left the car far from the entrance to not attract attention. He knew he was in enemy territory. But as a former military member, he had prepared himself for the worst. Nobody had seen him cross the frontward when he arrived at the entrance door. He went to the ring, and then he changed his mind. If his girlfriend's father happened to be there, no doubt that he was not going to let him in. He took the wall to the first floor, opened a window, and got inside the house. He glanced furtively into different rooms before they fell on Joyce's. She was sleeping, her face was livid. She looked like she cried all the tears in her body. Ray sat down on a chair next to the bed and started watching over her with adulation.

The presence of a car parked in this peaceful street seemed suspicious for the neighbors. It's never happened before. One of them called John Gallagher who called the police himself. Ray was looking at the sleeping girl when her father got angrily in her room followed by two policemen. They robbed their weapons immediately on Ray. He immediately raised slowly his hands in the air and made them understand that he was not armed and that he hadn't meant to resist. But Gallagher asked them to kill that son of a bitch. They hesitated. It was the noise that awakened Joyce. Instinctively, she jumped out the bed and threw in between the police and her boyfriend. She told her father, strong-minded, "If you kill him, you'll have to kill me too." But Gallagher was angry that the police had no intention of carrying out his orders. So he rushed to his room to arm himself with a rifle. At that time came a second police vehicle. Roy and his teammate jumped anxiously on the first floor, and they were nose to nose with John Gallagher. They asked him to drop the weapon on the ground. But this one refused. For an answer, he hurled abusive and racist remarks at Ray. Even his daughter was blamed with a racist remark. Gallagher's behavior put the policemen in an embarrassing position. If this behavior wasn't uncontrolled, the situation would have already been circumscribed for a long time.

The yells warned Mary Gallagher who rushed in her daughter room. Two minutes later, it was the four rednecks who rushed into the room too. Apart from Joyce's mother, everyone had a gun on Joyce who used her body to protect Ray. Then she had become furious and raged with allegations against this gang of racists as she qualified them. It was Mary

Gallagher and Roy who, by dint of persuasion, managed to calm the rednecks and John. The deputy chief of police unsheathed his revolver and ordered the other policemen to do the same. As law enforcement, he decided to confiscate all weapons. He put the handcuffs in Ray's hands and asked everyone to step aside. The tone he employed made it clear that he was not joking. The expression of his face had also changed. He had to end that disgraceful scene. It was the opposite of all that he had learned during his life as a soldier and a police officer. That day too, John Gallagher lost all consideration he had for him.

During all that, Ray had never lost his calm temper. He had said absolutely nothing. When it was time to leave after being handcuffed, he stared at Joyce's eyes and gave her apologies and begged her to take care of her. He said at the end that she didn't have to worry and everything would be fine. Then he made a gesture of honor of the head to Mary Gallagher and allowed himself to be guided by Roy as he walked in the middle of the police toward the exit.

Ray was embedded in Roy's vehicle. The sound of the police sirens had alerted the neighbors. Some had even armed themselves with their rifles in case to support the Gallaghers. When Ray arrived at the police station, he was taken to the interrogation room. After a briefing with the four police officers, the police chief interrogated the accused of about thirty minutes in the presence of Roy. Then he drove him into a cell. After this interrogation, he did not know where to begin to write his report. He could no longer disregard the abduction of Joyce by the four rednecks, these members of the group far right that also had been already arrested, on several times, for violence against women. He couldn't also forget the events of Thanksgiving and the fact that all Arab city already knew about the relationship between Ray and Joyce. He didn't want the prosecutor of Montgomery investigating this story. What was still worrying him more than anything was that the NACCP and the press were affected by this case. That would be a disaster. The intent of the police chief was to avoid a scandal. His son who was his deputy warned him that he wasn't going to give up its future to save John Gallagher or forgot his own obligations for his friend and brotherhood.

Ray spent the night in the office of the chief of the Arab police station. Roy had insisted on that point, and his father was in his side. There was no question that his friend was locked in a cell. In light of the events, he didn't deserve it. But no one wanted to attract the wrath of John Gallagher by releasing the cumbersome accused so quickly.

In the same evening, Roy himself removed Ray's vehicle and parked it at the police station, fearing that his captain could be targeted for retribution by Gallagher's supporters. Before going home, Roy had a brief conversation with Ray. He reassured him of his loyalty while explaining the complexity of the situation. "We will find a solution very quickly, I give you my word," he had told him by turning his back.

Once at home, Roy called to rescue the commander of his ex-division at the special forces. He was still in service. This one had a paternal affection for Ray. He asked him to act discreetly. He was aware that John Gallagher could call on politicians to Montgomery and pressure the chief of police that the case could go further. This man had lost his sense of reason. He could do anything, even if it should lead him to ruin. His hatred was stronger.

Col. Norman Krupp prepared to go to Washington in the Department of Defense for a major appointment when he received Roy's phone call. He soon asked his secretary to postpone the meeting because he had to go to Arab city that night. An incident of extreme importance awaited him. He immediately left his office in uniform and took the direction to Arab in an army vehicle. He was accompanied by three officers, real warriors who seemed to be coming out of the expendables catalog. He drove all night in order to arrive at his destination first hour in the morning. When they arrived at the police station, the policemen on duty were surprised to see them coming. It was as if they saw aliens. This was a picture that they see in the movies as Colonel Krupp was alongside with his two giant Black men who looked like a SWAT team commando.

The police chief arrived five minutes later and warned by one officer. Colonel Krupp presented himself with courtesy but with the accent of a true adventurer. He gave him a handshake that made him feel a little pain. He asked to speak to his man. The expression surprised the policeman.

The latter pretended not to be impressed, but in his insides, he worried about the turn that took the events because he was witnessing too much. When Ray found himself in front of his ex-chief, he looked surprised. He raised from the chair where he had spent the night seated, to put himself in a stretch. "Colonel," he said.

"Captain. Rest. I see that you hadn't used the couch," said Krupp.

"No, Colonel, I was keeping my battle station."

Krupp laughed at the joke. "You're going to have to practice this before you get married." The chief of police smiled in turn. He really didn't know that his son was part of a brotherhood that defied the limits of friendship to the point that no sacrifice was enough. Although he knew that this was all his work, he was proud to see how much he surpassed it. Since the beginning of this whole affair, he had not stopped to impress him.

Col. Norman Krupp spent twenty minutes one on one with Ray. Meanwhile, the other soldiers stayed outside with their former comrade, Roy Wilkins Junior. It was admirable! The latter had recovered his memories and his buddies. As time passed, the office resumed most of its daily activities.

After his conversation with Ray, Colonel Krupp left the office to go and talk with the police chief who was waiting for him at Roy's office. When the two men were face-to-face, their expression spoke of themselves. They were the same age, and they understood each other easily. "We have to let him go right now," said the military.

"I see no disadvantage," said the policeman, "but I have obligations. I have to call some people before making a final decision. Like you, Colonel, I have obligations."

The police chief called immediately the judge, the mayor, and John Gallagher for an urgent meeting with the colonel. The latter, by learning of Colonel Krupp's presence in Arab city and his men, was frankly surprised. He wondered, on his way to this appointment, how a military senior officer of the army was concerned by a simple case of forced entry as far from his military base. It was an outcome that he did not expect.

When he crossed the police station parking lot, he had a glimpse of the soldiers chatting with Roy. It did not bode well for him. When he pulled the door from the police chief's office, he was anxious. The others were waiting for him. The five men discussed together for an hour without releasing any friendliness to one another. They were unhappy listening to Colonel Krupp spit out the truth about this case. He offered them an honorable outing by asking them to release Ray without condition. In back, he'd ask him not to communicate the case to the press and NACCP or to bring a lawsuit against anyone. He assured them that Ray wouldn't do anything that could hurt Roy or his family and friends.

The judge actually believed that there was no need to prosecute the case. The chief of police seized the opportunity to disengage. John Gallagher, feeling isolated, accepted sadly this decision at only one condition that Ray doesn't ever come back again at Arab and never try to see his daughter. There was a silence into the room for a minute. Then the colonel stood up and said loudly, "No, never. It's something that a military cannot accept. There's a limit to not cross." On this, he turned his back after a military salute.

After Colonel Krupp's departure, the four men remained together for five minutes. The police chief took the opportunity to say to John Gallagher that they all had the interest to finish with this story as soon as possible. He believed Ray was quite correct during this whole affair and that he firmly whispered that he wasn't going to make waves especially after the recommendations of his commander and because of Roy. John Gallagher didn't say a word. He gratified himself with shaking head. Then he stood up, disappointed, and left the room with the feeling of being humiliated.

John Gallagher had a coalface when he left the police station. As he walked toward his vehicle, his scrutiny crossed again, the soldiers and Roy in countless conversation. He didn't believe that the colossus that escorted Colonel Krupp knew how to laugh. They looked one another in unfamiliarity. Roy was happy to make him a gesture with the hand. He had been caught short by the behavior of the latter that he had always wished have to be his stepfather.

When the police chief pulled the doors from his desk, Ray was standing in front of the window and looked at the tree movements by the wind. He was lost in his thoughts when the noise of the steps made him turn his head. "Mister Ray, I think you can give back my office. You are free to go," he said, trying to be nice. "I had no idea, my debt to you. Thank you very much for everything. I understand why my son respects you so much." "Your son!" exclaimed Ray, surprised.

"Yes, Roy is my son, and I entrust to you the secret that he was the eternal lover of Joyce since teenage. That is why he had not yet married to another woman, but she loves you. Sorry for all this." He shook Ray's hand with a bit of regret, touched his shoulder, and congratulated him with good luck before he let him go.

Ray arrived at the police station main entrance tired. It was with emotion that he faced his military comrades. He hadn't seen them for years. They did not stop congratulating themselves with so much spirit that they troubled the tranquility of the place. It was Roy who intervened to offer them to go and continue the conversation in front of their lunch. They walked to his father's restaurant near to the police station. The manager was also an ex-Navy Seal at the same platoon who Roy had called to come to Arab city to take away from the posttraumatic problems after his withdrawal from the army. Finally, there would be, at least in Arab city, a story where Black people did not seem like a lowlife.

CHAPTER 10
THE UNEXPECTED OUTCOME

Joyce became hysterical when the police arrested Ray in front of her. She started to scream with all her strength and to overthrow everything that was within her grasp. She had become uncontrollable in spite of her mother's supplications. Finally, on the order of her father, it was the four rednecks who immobilized her. When she was unable to react, she spurred a crisis and fell unconscious. For once, her mother panicked. She was lying on the bed totally unmoving. At this time, the attendance of Alison seemed more than necessary. She would know immediately what to do without to call the emergency. But she was far from Arab with her children and grandchildren. John Gallagher, in hurriedness, called his personal doctor. Fortunately, he was at home. He brought himself his medical kit. He made her go back to her and prescribed calming that one of the rednecks ran to buy at the pharmacy. Joyce took a pill and fell asleep five minutes later. Soon after, a deep peacefulness invaded the house. It was like someone had just died.

Joyce had not left the house since her abduction. She had tried out on twice, but the rednecks had prevented it. Her father never showed, and her mother got back to her habits with her friends. During this time, she had become depressed. She had lost appetite. She hoped, however, that her father would become rational and that subsequently she could decide her future. She wished to leave the house at the first opportunity and to resume her life with Ray at Montgomery or West Palm Beach because she loved his family so much. For now, unable to call because she didn't have access to any phone, she gave the impression to her family that she had turned the page.

Until John Gallagher had recalled Alison to look after her, Joyce did speak to nobody else. That's why she was the only one who knew that she hadn't had her period for two months at least. Far from panicking, she saw in this event an exit door. She didn't expect that her father would force her to have an abortion. His faith did not allow it. Her only support was Roy's visits. They weren't talking about Ray. She still did not know that the two men had very strong friendships. That's why she was amazed to see that he had not tempted to seduce her. At the contrary, he did his best to comfort her. Mary Gallagher encouraged his visits and began to hope that could change in a love story.

That day, it was Joyce's birthday. Since three months cut off from the outside world, she hadn't heard from Ray. Her concern grew to become melancholic. She was scared and bored by the reactions of her father. Her boyfriend either decided to abandon her. She still didn't have her period, and finally, thanks to Alison who had bought a pregnancy test kit, she knew for sure now that she was pregnant. Time began to be long.

For this birthday, Joyce wanted only one thing: Ray. Addicted by force in her own house, she was getting tired. She noted that home monitoring wasn't relaxed. Instead, her father brought two German shepherds, and wire fences were installed around the house. Now to get the front yard, everybody had to ring the bell at one hundred meters from the house and wait for the guard to avoid being devoured by the dogs who patrolled twenty-four hours a day. If it wasn't for Alison's affections, she would have succumbed into total depression. At least she was a person to pamper her. It was her who called Roy to prepare, at least, a small party with friends for her birthday. Indeed, in the early evening, Roy came with chocolate cake and a gift that he had drawn from his personal affairs. Joyce protested in vain. But Roy had insisted that she had to save her energy for later because he planned to spend the evening with her and their childhood friends who were in the town. When the night fell, Roy started a fire of wood on the courtyard and sat up some chairs around for the dozen people present. Alison proposed to bring them something to eat.

Joyce opened the gifts she had from her friends, Alison, her mother, and even her father who had sent her a great picture of them when she was five years old. But when she opened that one from Roy, she was struck with wonder. Indeed, he had offered him a box containing CD's of several Haitian musical groups. She hadn't controlled herself. She jumped upon him to kiss him as a big brother. He couldn't imagine how that gift was special. "How did you know, Roy?" asked Joyce.

"Hum," said Roy, "you not going to believe it. Ray and I have known each other for years. He was my boss when I was in Navy Seal, and I thank him that I'm alive." A reflect of joy was immediately on Joyce's face for the first time. Despite his persistence, he gave her no news of Ray. He had promised his father to not interfere in this story for some reason. He told her about their personal relationships in brief and became quiet.

The young woman realized she couldn't go any further and changed the conversation as she had to avoid indiscretions in front of her guests.

Joyce stood up and changed the CD in the unit who previously played Jazz to add Haitian music. The rhythm put immediately some hot ambiance in that gloomy party. It's RAM. Roy explained to his friends that it was a band led by an American/Haitian that lived in Port-au-Prince who played a mixture of rock and voodoo. Then he began to tell them the story of Richard Morse and his passage to the Hotel Oloffson in Haiti where this band gave every Thursday night an exceptional show. But Roy did not explain that he had already made several missions to this country with Ray to stop several Haitian and Colombian drug dealers or to protect the American Embassy during periods of turbulence.

While his friends were drinking beer, Joyce took some lemonade and even tried to tell an old childhood joke. When the atmosphere became more joyful, Roy set alight the candles of the cake and solicited the attention of all. Before the concerned do the breath, he made a three-minute speech and asked everybody to sing "Happy Birthday." Everyone made oaths as discreet as possible to avoid raising suspicion on what they were already presenting. Joyce blew out the candles, took a knife, and cut the first little piece. She plunged her little spoon into the chocolate cake to draw a bite that she bore to her mouth with her usual grace. She barely swallowed it when she began to gasp. She grew insipid suddenly. Then it was a sticky jet coming out of her mouth. She had started to vomit abundantly. Her friends panicked. Called by the general fear, Alison arrived quickly to help her got better. She made her shake the water in her mouth, washed her face, and asked Roy to carry her in his arms to her room. She was sweaty and trembled in a fever. She looked Roy in the eyes and said, "Ray, it's you!" Then she fell unconscious. Alison called 911 immediately, even she was in her higher emotion. A few minutes later, an ambulance was driving her to Marshall Medical Center North. When the medical team arrived, Alison began to cry and insisted to ride in the ambulance. If it wasn't for the intervention of Roy, who offered to take her to the hospital, she should be arrested by the police who arrived at the same time. She had clung to the vehicle.

Joyce regained consciousness at the hospital before her mother's arrival. Alison was at her bedside as well as her friend's. Fortunately, there was more fear than that. The first tests did not reveal anything abnormal. She was pretty healthy. For the doctor, the sudden vomiting and unconsciousness weren't intoxication but to something that was already in her before she ate the piece of cake, that he proposed her to discover with a pregnancy test. A few minutes later, he confirmed what Joyce already knew. When she received the news, she was with Alison in the room. She tried to comfort her. They knew that would not be easy to give the bad news to John Gallagher. She imagined already that he would be devastated as he hated Ray. But for her mother, she predicted that she would take it with philosophy. They had never been close. Even Joyce was confident that her father would not force her to have an abortion because of his faith, she decided to inform her friends that were still in the waiting room of the hospital, a way to avoid the stupidities of her father. Most people knew, most that she could prevent her dad's misconduct.

John Gallagher arrived at the hospital in the early morning, so his wife and Alison were still at the bedside of Joyce. His four thugs were at his side. He was already informed of the reason that had led his daughter in the emergency room. He didn't even see her in the room. He already knew that before the end of the day, all Arab city would already be informed that her daughter was pregnant for a fucking Negro. But it was something that very few people should see. He offered to take the necessary measures accordingly.

It was noon when Joyce was allowed to leave the hospital. When she rose from the chair to the exit, two vehicles in tinted glass were waiting for her. Alison and Mary Gallagher were forced to take place in one of the vehicles with two of the rednecks while Joyce was escorted by the two others in another vehicle. Instead of taking the direction of the house at Arab, it was a mountain road they took. Joyce was ravished. She looked behind her to check if the other vehicle was always following them. At least she was guaranteed that she would not make her disappear. No one spoke. Two hours later, the vehicles stopped in a mountain manor isolated from any other housings. It looked like a spot of secret agents. Even Mary Gallagher ignored that her husband owned this cottage like a Swiss chalet. So far, in several opportunities, the future of Montgomery and the American elections for all the state of Alabama was decided in this place. Senators, congressmen, members of the legislative assembly of the state, members of the Republican Party, businessmen, and members of the Ku Klux Klan had gone through this. But with the arrival of Democrats to power and the Chinese commercial competition, business was less good, and John Gallagher was losing influence. So the place wasn't longer frequented for some time, but it had kept all its beauty because two people were permanently in charge for the maintenance.

The three women were greeted by the guardians of the place with their usual courtesy. They did not know them and should never seek to identify them. For them, the rules were the same: you don't see anything, and you don't hear anything. Juggling four helped their prisoners to settle down and were taking rooms in bungalows of the residence. The women could circulate as they wanted, even go into the woods. But in the middle of nowhere, it was impossible for them to escape. There was no dwelling in the vicinity, no phone, no other road. They should have real courage and a lot of tips to avoid the cameras that watched the surroundings and especially have the resilience to escape. But the three women hadn't these abilities.

The house was exceptionally well decorated. There were pictures of Joyce everywhere and very little of her mother. Her life was on the walls, in the many photos albums and video recordings. Her meetings with Ray and some of their privacy in the apartment or they had lived were there. Joyce found all memories of her life, even those that recall the moments where her father was absent. It was her personal museum with all the books she had already read, the movies that she had watched, and unexpectedly the memories of her trip to Haiti. Joyce thought rightly that her father had to know a CIA agent who worked at the embassy in Haiti and even hired a private investigator to watch her since childhood. She had found even his bag with his notebook she had lost at the Montgomery airport after returning from vacation in Haiti. She was, at the same time, honored and petrified. She had never imagined this side—passionate, dark, and evil—of her father. This swelled secretly jealous of her mother who made the admonition as if her daughter was the only love of her husband life and that she was the woman who was carrying his child.

The three women had found all those they needed to live in that isolated place of the rest of the world such as a luxurious kitchen with their favorite foods, containing rooms, and clothes which they might need. But there were also games, dozens of channels of satellite TV, and sport and cinema room. A doctor came every two weeks to see them, especially to follow Joyce's pregnancy. But John never came for the time that the three women were in this house. None of their personal friends either. Nobody, by the way, knew where they were.

Isolation allowed the mother and daughter to confess to each other, to forgive themselves, to reconcile, and to develop their friendship of solidarity. Alison was the center of this change. Mary Gallagher had ended up also by considering her as a big sister than as an ex-nanny. She realized that racial discrimination had obscured her judgment against that Black woman, this same demon who pushed her husband to keep them trapped in this isolated house on the surveillance of men who, in her eyes, saw the women as a private property of their husbands.

Joyce had become the best friend of her mother. Unmistakable complicity brought the three women together. Now the time seemed to them to be less long and their daily life more bearable. Mary Gallagher was also cured of her jealousy. Joyce found her mother to the point of making Alison jealous. Her pregnancy became an admiration for these two mothers. This conviviality had also affected the sensitivity of the rednecks even to Alison. They started little by understanding each other to make revelations on the secret activities of many people of Arab city.

This night, Mary Gallagher had invited the guardians and the rednecks at Alison's birthday snack. In the privacy of the moment, those men had become sympathetic. Since their arrival, Alison had fed them well, cleaned their clothes, and even they had told stories. They had talked about their families, their lives, and their conditions of existence. Unexpectedly, they had found common ground: poverty and under education that had made them vulnerable citizens of second zones, influenced by powerful people and politicians.

This birthday was a true moment of happiness and surprise. It was Mary Gallagher who made the chocolate cake, and these were the rednecks, excited by whiskey, which first began to sing the happy birthday. Joyce also sang with cheerfulness. She had found a bit of happiness. She stood up to make a speech when she immediately felt a slight pain and something that flowed from her feet. She stopped talking when she felt that she broke the waters. Alison understood immediately and took control of the situation. One of the rednecks jumped on a vehicle to ride to the doctor. In the meantime, Alison made her ready to give birth the baby in case the doctor did not arrive on time. That's what happened ninety minutes later. Indeed, Joyce had given birth to a pretty healthy little boy. When the baby was in her arms, light flew from the eyes of the child that pulled out some tears from Mary Gallagher's eyes. She was the happiest grandma in the world. She did not expect to be a grandmother at fifty years of such a beautiful baby. Alison was just as proud. She had just given birth to the second baby of the family on the very day of her birthday. It was her best gift.

Joyce was excited about the birth of her son. For now, nobody could tell who he looked like. But for Mary Gallagher, he was the exact image of his grandfather and that he was the boy that he waited for and she hadn't been able to give to him to preserve the family's name. At the same time, she was concerned about her husband's feedback because so far he was doing everything to avoid Joyce.

John Gallagher learned of the birth of the baby while he was in his office at Montgomery in the midst of torment. The bank had just cut off definitely all credits, and shareholders, partners, and friends threatened to liquidate their parts in the industry. They had told him kindly, at the first offer, they would sell their shares if a solution was not found in the days to come. This did not prevent him to cancel all his appointments and return to Arab city. In the evening, he invited his closest friends: the judge, the police chief, the mayor, his pastor, and the leader of the far white in a meeting at home. He had to find a solution to prevent Ray to be knowledgeable about the birth and avoid his daughter to pretend to give him the paternity. His friends proposed to help him at the condition to avoid any violence and disgrace.

The mayor advised John to register the child at the town hall as being his son. He would arrange to do that without any problem. But it was only him who made the decision to keep his daughter away from Montgomery and the country. Ray shouldn't ever learn about the birth of the child or the place where his daughter lived. The three women should not be informed of what was going to be decided between them. There was still having to set the place where Joyce would be sent. It was the pastor who proposed to play his influences within the hierarchy of the Catholic Church of Montgomery. In fact, at the beginning of the civil rights movement, some priests had linked with some fundamentalist Protestant backgrounds against the Black movement. A secret agreement had unified them until the proclamation of 1964 Civil Rights Act by President Johnson. But this law had never been really applied in Arab city since there were almost no Black people at the time. The agreement had been dissolved by itself by those priests who had taken, in part, the head of some clergymen districts of the state. Others had voluntarily immigrated to South Africa to serve the apartheid movement. The pastor had kept his contacts and had made trips in this country on several occasions.

The pastor called a powerful priest friend in Montgomery to ask him to bring the girl to a friend in a convent in South Africa without giving information on the situation. He hadn't called the bishop directly in order to not provide more explanations. If it came from a least important religious authority, it attracted less attention. The prelate asked him for a week to give him an answer. This was not the first time they sent to exile a young girl who ignored their rules and the ultra-conservative white tradition. In this part of the Deep South, if some bad practices weren't anymore, some far-right White groups still directed the politics. They managed to protect themselves by controlling political, economic, and even policing power and justice. What they feared was to see the federal government delegate new FBI special agents to come interfering around their business. This had already happened in Montgomery on several occasions with negative consequences for their interests.

Two weeks later, John Gallagher received the phone call he was expecting. A place was released for Joyce in the convent of Sacred Heart at Ixopo, a small town in the southwest of Durban. The same evening, he sent a message to his rednecks to bring everybody to Arab city. It was with pleasure that the women were taking the road home with the baby without suspecting what was waiting for them. Joyce proposed, when she arrived, to make the birth statement mother of the child on behalf of Ray Gaillard Gallagher while waiting to contact Ray.

Ixopo was the opposite of Arab city. It was a small town located In KwaZulu-Natal in South Africa with a population of 12,000 persons with 90 percent Black and 1.4 percent White. This minority part of the population was of German and English origins. The rest of the population consisted of people of colors and emigrants coming from India in particular and from all over Asia. The White community considered themselves as superior to others. He maintained direct contact with other communities because that was the only way to do business with them. Otherwise, there was no common ground even in God. He established link of solidarity and relations since several years with far-right White of Arab and Montgomery in their fight against Nelson Mandela and Martin Luther King. It was first and foremost the White supremacists beyond religious practices.

Arriving in Arab city, Alison returned to her room. It was a quite comfortable building where Joyce had spent her childhood and adolescence with her. She naturally expected the baby to be having the same from her.

Joyce, from her side, went up to her room with her baby that she fed only with maternal milk. In the evening, Alison had prepared her favorite food that she was getting ready to serve her at the bed. But when she arrived in front of the chamber, one of the rednecks barred the road nicely and proposed to do so himself. It was John Gallagher's order, he told her. She insisted in vain, but the redneck contended. Finally, two others arose behind her, took the meal from her hands, and made her walk down the stairs. John Gallagher and a doctor were waiting for the plate in the contiguous room. They had already prepared her dose of Valium which he added in the cup of tea and in the water bottle that accompanied. Joyce hesitated before to accept it. The server looked embarrassed, but he finally told him that she was in her father's house and that nothing could happen to her. In the face of the young mother's hesitation, he laid the tray on the bedside table and wished her good appetite and the good night before turning back. Joyce drank a cup of tea and ignored the food. She took the book that she had begun to read and lay down on the bed. Five minutes later, she drowsed already insistently, and her eyes couldn't stay open. She drank some water to quench her sudden thirst. She had no idea when she was struck by sleep.

It was the noise of the engines and the turbulence that woke her up twelve hours later. She opened her eyes slowly to see with amazement that she was lying on a chair in a plane, the belt perfectly attached. She uttered a cry that startled the other occupants who had snoozed off. In this jet that a friend had borrowed for her father, no one paid attention to her. The three security guards looked at her indifferently and then turned her head. One of the pilots went in and asked if everything was okay. The security guards made a gesture, and then he returned to the cabin. Nobody spoke to her or brought attention to her tears.

The airplane made three stops during the trip before landing at Durban twenty-four hours later after she left Montgomery. She rolled on the tarmac to go park in an isolated hangar from the airport. Two 1970 Land Rover vehicles were waiting for her. There was no question or passing the customs. Joyce was forced to go down and settle in one of the vehicles in the middle of two South African White men. Her bodyguards were carrying her luggage in the other vehicle. The little convoy took an exit to engage in a road which led to Ixopo. The pilots were immediately on the plane and flew to Montgomery without worrying about what was going to happen.

The two Land Rover rolled full throttle to their destination without care about the prisoner. They did not know her or any desire to engage any conversation with her. Joyce didn't even have the courage to ask where she was and where they took her. This was no more important. She looked at the scenery passing before her eyes as a world away from her native Alabama and her country. The environment, the scorching heat, and these rough and frankly rude White men had nothing to do with Americans. She said to herself that she was going to be patient and smart to survive in this exile that her father confined to her. She told herself that if her father had the courage to do so with her only child out of hatred for a Black man, perhaps, the rumors circulating accusing him having participated in lynching Black people were true. Then her mind turned to Ray from whom she was without news and especially to her son that she was forced to give up without having time to kiss the last time. She made a choice to live for them and to focus her efforts to see them again. She decided to play the game while waiting to find the way out.

When Joyce crossed the barrier in this convent, she felt that she was changing century. She found herself inside a convent with young girls dressed like those of Saudi Arabia. She suspected that she was not alone in this situation. As she dropped away from the vehicle, a small bell rang the twelve knocks of midday. Soon, she heard a humming choir of Gregorian chant. It was solemn and soothing. She closed her eyes to let her breach by the softness of these harmonious and gentle voices. In the bliss of the moment after the emotions of these latest hours, she hadn't seen this great lady with the rigid face that walked toward her. "Hello and welcome, Sister Marie Anne, at the Sacred Heart Ixopo Convent. I am Sister Elisabeth, the superior. Follow me in my office, please." Then she turned her back on her. She had almost answered as she was surprised to learn her new name. But as she had decided to play the game, she didn't.

Entering the office of the superior, Sister Marie Anne felt through internal peace. So she listened quietly to the recommendations and agreed to respect the rules of the institution. She could not communicate with the outside world under any circumstances and would not have access to any uselessness. She had no right on the phone, television, or radio station. She would have to pray three times a day, take part in religious training, and work on production management. The administration proposed to give her a new ID without indication of 1556 nationality until her religious education was completed.

Joyce hadn't asked any questions and didn't worry about anything. Since no one didn't seem to know the story of her life and did not seem to care, she decided to remain in complete silence.

CHAPTER 11

THE AVATARS OF LIFE

Ten days after Joyce had been banished from Arab city, John Gallagher brought his wife, for the first time since more than two years, to a fancy restaurant in Montgomery. He wished to be forgiven and reconcile with her for good. His pastor had insisted to him to start a process of renewal that would end on the day that his daughter would return from her banishment. He told him that he had sent Joyce in Australia with friends until people forget that history. John Gallagher Jr., the name he had given the baby, would be their legitimate child. Alison, as she had done in the last few days, would be responsible for taking care of the child, he said at the end of the conversation. He apologized for his bad behavior and gave her a guarantee that their life would have something merry. She listened in silence as usual and contented herself with not breaking the enchantment that seemed to be born. She made the choice to accommodate without giving up the new feelings she worshipped now to her daughter. She said to herself that she was going to try to convince her husband to bring back their daughter as soon as possible.

That night, after dinner, the Gallaghers started a new honeymoon. They were making love for the first time since more than a year. Mary Gallagher had this ability to adapt to all situations. She enjoyed the changes and started new maternity. Little Junior, as they called the baby now, brought a fresh air at the house. For the moment, he seemed to be a true White boy. He had the skin of his mother that hid his Afro origin, something that his grandfather considered as a blessing from heaven.

Despite the continuous decline of his businesses, John Gallagher gave himself also a new chance in a lifetime. Junior had changed his horizons and projections. He had found his paternity attractions. The little boy was in his legs whenever he was at home. From time to time, Alison became jealous when he spent too much time in the hands of his grandparents, on the pretext of late baths or late meals. When John spent time at Montgomery, Alison, his wife, and baby Junior joined him on Wednesday and came back with him every Friday at Arab city. The family had finally so much hope for the boy. When the time had come to present him at the temple, it was Roy who was designated to be the godfather. It was an honor that he had accepted with joy. He had made the trip from Washington only for the ceremony. Since earlier one year, he had found a new job in the office of the secretariat of veterans after the sponsorship of a senator. He owed it to John Gallagher who made him elected. They should have taken Roy away from Montgomery. He had become too liberal for the clan.

The business of John Gallagher had deteriorated that made him fire employees for the first time. Until he's no longer having access to the credits, he asked the bank to help him find new investors as well to be able to buy new equipment and pay his debts. All his former partners and friends had turned his back on him. They no longer believed in a recovery and were losing money. All they wanted was to sell as soon as possible before it's too late. John Gallagher needed at least $6 million ASAP; otherwise, he would be totally bankrupt in three months.

Brian Donovan was in his New York office at Manhattan when he got a call from his friend Greg Colson, former marine like him, who worked at the bank that used John Gallagher. The next morning, he flew to Montgomery. Greg had come to pick him up at the airport and briefed him as he was heading to John Gallagher's factory. For two hours, the three men engaged a nonstop discussion on financial needs, strengths, weaknesses, perspectives, and especially on partnership. Brian had been reviewing all aspects of the problem by questioning the director, the production managers, human resources, and distribution. He made him communicate the recovery plan so he could study as quickly as possible.

Brian spent twenty-four hours at Montgomery to take note of the record and to investigate on the factory and its director. As he believed that was a good deal, he finally decided to invite Ray before leaving at the restaurant of the Staybridge Suites at 8:30 p.m. to talk about it. Brian had to apologize twice before the protests of Ray which reproached him for keeping him from coming. He would have facilitated him with things better than anyone else. But clarified Brian to him, he wouldn't link business with friendship. Then he explained to him the case and the investigation he led during the past forty-eight hours before making the decision to talk to him. In the end, without even waiting for the reaction of Ray, he proposed him to take control of the factory of John Gallagher as a majority shareholder. "For this," said Brian, "I need your permission to invest $10 million. This will give you 57 percent of the company with the purchase of some parts of Gallagher and of the totality of minority shareholders. The money will, among others, buy new equipment, pay debts, and renovate the building. I have studied all aspect of the project that Joyce had made for her father and I found it viable." By mentioning Joyce's name, Brian was waiting for a reaction from Ray. And that was exactly the case. He immediately saw his face contract in a way as if he woke up in him a bittersweet nostalgia.

Ray listened to Brian's explanations without asking any questions. He had full confidence in his judgment. The question was to know if he should get on an adventure involving John Gallagher after what happened. Money seemed not the main aspect for him. It would be several months that he had no news of Joyce despite repeated efforts. Even Roy would not talk to him about Joyce. Then he rose from the table, apologized to Brian, and took over the toilets. He washed his face and took the time to think before returning with his friend. "I have conditions to be satisfied before I accept," he said. John Gallagher should never know where the money came. "In fact, no one else will have to know. John Gallagher must remain the director with a signed power of attorney. The second high position must stay empty until Joyce gets back. John and you will have hands free to ensure the success of the reforms." Then he asked Brian to pass at other things. He quickly understood that

Ray had a gaping wound in the heart that would take time to rebuild. So it was not worth to raise subjects that hurt. He had learned to accept the misfortune of life. In his case, it was always the time that always brought the right solutions.

CHAPTER 12
THE STEEP PATH OF THE RENAISSANCE

Two years passed since Ray took the majority share in John Gallagher's factories. About 75 percent of his investment had already reimbursed back while business flourished. He had become the richest who graduated from Alabama University. He didn't give any sign of his fortune. He always lived in the same apartment in Montgomery that he had bought after selling his house in Florida. But he traveled a lot inside the United States to photograph exotic sites, one of his passions other than electronics. After his graduation, he took some time before going abroad on a professional activity.

That week, she was passing through New York and roamed in the Big Apple. He's always been attracted to Broadway and the musicals. He decided to go and see a greater number of possible shows before continuing his path. One morning, he went to see Brian at his office in Manhattan unannounced. He invited him for lunch in a small restaurant before he took the train to the Grand Canyon Park in Arizona. It looked like he was looking for the escape to drown his grief. For a successful man like him, spending two years in sexual abstinence, it was a record. What his friend had understood when he informed him of his plan was to extend his three month trip across the country. "Ray," said Brian, "you're going to change your life. The money is completely laundered. The compensations that you had after your many accidents and your investments can alone allow you a comfortable life. You could also open a company on Internet or own an information exchange site. With what you have, you could do everything that you want. The time has come for you to tidy up, to have woman, children, a dog, whatever. But you should change now. You can't go on like this. It will kill you with little fire."

But in spite of the insistence, Ray refused to hear anything. He had repressed on himself to the point of worry same as his parents. In front of the stiffening from his friend, Brian advised him to complete his journey of three months across the country and that before his return, he would ask his Montgomery real estate agent to look for him a beautiful house in a small town where he could keep his privacy while indulging in his passions.

"You accept my proposals, or I call Colonel Krupp."

"Okay," he answered him, bursting with laughter like a kid.

John Gallagher was a happy man. His life had changed dramatically since this last month. His business prospered more than he had hoped. He had returned to normal family life, and his little boy called him Papa. Everyone agreed to congratulate him because his grandson was his portrait spit. Politicians, businessmen, and old friends who let him down three years ago ran after him again. But he knew that he owed his good fortune to a mysterious investor whom he urged Brian, in vain, to make him meet. He was prepared to give him a very enticing proposal, feeling vulnerable to being indebted to someone who could, at any time, take control of a company founded by his grandparents. Finally, he planned a trip to South Africa to meet his daughter in order to begin the process of reconciliation of which her pastor asked urgently to advance.

After his journey through some states, Ray came back to Montgomery less stressed. His meeting with an Indian tribe had metamorphosed him. Three days later, it was him who called Brian about this house he had to buy. Brian was happy that his friend made up his mind. So he traveled to Montgomery the following Friday and proposed to spend the weekend with his fiancée and came back to New York City early Monday morning to go straight to his office. Before he left New York, he had made an appointment by phone with Lys Kay, the realtor who was harassing him for two months about this good deal frozen because of an invisible client.

Ray met Brian and his fiancée in the hotel restaurant on the very evening of their arrival in Montgomery. They exchanged the banalities of their lives, politics, and the bad jokes of the army. Fortunately, the girl was the type to impose herself in a conversation; otherwise, she would have been frankly angry and jealous to hear about the two men on things that shouldn't make her interested. But she was the kind, playful, and good journalist. She was immediately interested in the story of Ray's life. Brian had not stopped talking about him since their first meeting. She even proposed to write a book about him. So she pushed the conversation until the name Joyce emerged. As soon as Ray took a bathroom break, a diplomatic way to change conversation had to be done, and Brian had immediately understood. Fortunately, the realtor spent a good time. That made them change the conversation.

Lys Kay was not only a smart and beautiful woman, but also she was silhouette that they only meet in magazines. Knowing the madness of men for girls of her kind, she did her best to make them crazy for the only purpose of manipulating them. She was not at all an easy woman, but she never missed the opportunity to use her charm to make her business work. And it was really flourishing—her knowledge and her brazenly bullying men. So she only waited for those who were sufficiently open-minded to look at her as a person before her sexuality. But tonight, she had noticed that among the men in the restaurant, only Ray did not look to be impressed with her arrival. That had frankly surprised her. She proposed to get an idea of the specimen before deciding to try to seduce him.

"So you're the mysterious Ray," said Lys after the greetings of use.

"Absolutely not," answered Ray, giving her a kiss on the hand. "I am only the man to convince."

"Ah, replied this one. I will work on it. For starter, I have something that will probably please you."

The spontaneous laughter of Ray and Brian made the young woman blush. Having noticed the funniest of this response, she looked charmed by the quick laugh. To avoid a second time, she went straight to the point.

"I found a great property at Arab city, a Victorian style house with two acres of landscaped gardens and hundred-year-old trees for a low price and a paltry level of taxation. The house also has a comfortable apartment for caretakers, maids, and a studio for intellectual activities like painting, writing, or other. It's the city hall that sells."

"I'm sorry, but I'm absolutely not interested," said Ray without taking the time to listen to the end.

Lys was surprised by his hurried reaction.

"I think you should accept it," said Brian. "Even if I should invite our entire old platoon coming soon to watch out for, you shouldn't let go what had been haunting you all your life. We're military, man. Don't let it kill you."

"Lys," he said, "we'll make an appointment for tomorrow 8:30 in the morning to Arab city for a guided tour."

"And, Ray, stop protesting," said Brian. "Anyway, this will engage you in anything. After all these years, we became brothers. I should therefore allow me the right to interfere in your privacy if necessary and on certain occasions."

On this, they put an end to the conversation back to the joke, just to make laugh to Lys. They spent two or more hours before they split.

Early the next day, Brian took Ray home. He was amazed by the beauty of his house. He discovered for the first time an exotic and Caribbean world in Alabama. They took a coffee before leaving to Arab city. They took advantage of the moment to discuss business, their private lives, and the old comrades of the army and to remember bad jokes during some secret operations. Time passed so fast that Ray didn't notice that they were in the suburbs of Arab city. Certainly, he didn't remember having been down this road. That's why when Brian stopped before this house that he would visit, he wasn't focused on the property on the other side. Hardly, he had set foot on the property that Lys Kay gave him a hello with an expressive smile. She was really pleased that he came. She seemed to be paying special attention to Ray. Brian noticed it right away. He hoped that he could subsequently encourage them to move in a private relationship.

Ray had already a first good impression after a brief glance of the property. Seen from the outside, it was impressive. Lys proposed to him to go around before visiting the house and the other adjoining buildings. At this time, they saw blazing flames in a building of the opposite property. Ray and Brian ran immediately through the fences to answer a desperate call. Fortunately, there were no more dogs. When they arrived, the building where Alison lived was on fire. They entered to help the last tenants to go out through a window. At this second, they fell on John Gallagher who went out of the main house. Ray remained frozen one moment as if he had just seen a ghost. They looked in the eyes without moving while the flames spread. The cries of Alison made them come back and told them that Junior was still asleep in the dorm on the first floor. John Gallagher hadn't hesitated to cross the flames to pounce on the stairs in order to rescue his grandson. Before coming down, a part of the house had collapsed and blocked the passage to Ray who was trying to get through the flame too. They could hear the sirens of police and firefighters who were brought by far, but with the intensity of the fire, relief would have arrived too late. Suddenly, John Gallagher appeared through a window with the child wrapped in a blanket. Suddenly, Ray beckoned him to the drop that he did without hesitation. Junior was received in the arms of his real father without realizing it.

Then Ray and Brian had unwrapped the blanket in both ends to allow John to skip his turn to the window. Just as he prepared to begin, an explosion blew up the house. The two men were thrown at some yards back, safe and sound, but with a few minor burns. John Gallagher was not so lucky. He was sunk to the ground floor in the debris that burnt intently while firefighters rushed to extinguish the fire. His death was painful. It was total consternation.

Ray and Brian received first aid on the spot while waiting to go to the hospital for a full assessment. The paramedic service also assessed Junior and all the employees of the house. Firefighters and crime-scene investigating doctors and detectives began their investigation before the body was routed to Montgomery for forensic identification and autopsy.

The fire in the building and the death of John Gallagher created a shock throughout the neighborhood. There was no time to understand what had happened. The house was filled with people. It seemed that the whole city was meeting nearby on the property. He reined a morbid atmosphere. Mary Gallagher was devastated. It was Alison who took things in hand, especially to calm Junior who claimed his father.

Ray relived for the first time Mary Gallagher and friends that were the witnesses to this Thanksgiving dinner. It was a cordial but fulfilled suspicious gathering. But Ray felt that people hid him something as long as they looked embarrassed. The back and forth look of Alison between Junior and Ray made Mrs. Gallagher off. She had this feeling that the secret could not be kept for long. She eventually convinced themselves, in order to avoid another tragedy, to talk to him immediately. So without consulting any of her friends, she asked Ray to join her in private for a quick talk.

Ray followed Mary Gallagher in the kitchen under the interrogator look of the fifteen people still at home that undoubtedly were in secret. But they had no idea what kind of conversation they were going to have. She prepared two cups of tea, gave one to Ray, and asked him to sit down next to her as if they were old friends. She began by thanking him for being there and apologizing for what had happened during Thanksgiving Day also for the harm her family had caused him. "Ray," she said, "Junior is your son." He was already wary of the idea that Mary Gallagher wanted to talk to him, but he did not expect this news.

The shock was such that it spilled part of his tea. Then she took the time to calmly explain the history. Ray had become pale and unable to listen to more. He asked Mary Gallagher to show him the path to the bathroom because he needed to erase the lividity of his face and the tears that flowed from his eyes.

Ray came back from the toilet with a relaxed face because this news, in spite of everything, had made him a happy man. As he was going to take his place in front of her, Mary Gallagher gave him a long hug. She apologized again of all the pains the family had caused him. Then they talked again for about twenty minutes about the decisions to be made for the funeral and the return of Joyce without knowing that she was in South Africa and not in Australia.

Mary Gallagher confessed to Ray that she was going to have trouble managing her husband's business. In fact, she knew absolutely nothing about it. She counted on him to convince Joyce to take care of it when she returned. For now, she was lost. She did not know whether to ask for help from her husband's friends or to stop all the industry temporarily. The truth was, she was trying to ask him his assistance since they had now a common interest.

"Don't worry, Ms. Gallagher," reassured him. "Since two years, I own 57 percent of the company, and that was me who had decided, in the utmost secrecy, to let John Gallagher lead so as not to crumple his pride since Joyce had written the restructuring draft who saved her father from bankruptcy. With your permission," he said, "to put an end to this conversation, my financial agent will take care of it. There was a clause in the contract that allows me to solve the problem."

It was a big surprise for Mary Gallagher. It was too much emotion for her in one day. She decided to go up to her room to rest and left Alison to manage the people still present. Before she went away, Ray introduced her to Brian, and the three of them agreed to call John Gallagher's attorney to arrange a meeting at the company with the main supervisors and administrators. It was not necessary that the news of the death of the boss shocked the operation of a company.

Upon returning home in the evening, Ray could not sleep. He thought a great deal about Joyce and especially Junior huddled in his arms after catching him. The idea that John Gallagher could sacrifice his life for his child didn't seem to him to be obvious. This drama reminded him of how unpredictable human beings could be. He was thinking a lot about what he should do and especially when he met again with Joyce. To spend the time on that night that seemed so long, he prepared himself a rum punch as his father had taught him and slipped a record of Ella Fitzgerald in his phonograph. This night, he counted to spend it with closest friends like Billie Holiday, Sarah Vaughan, Aretha Franklin, Martha Jean-Claude, and Emerante de Pradines.

Mary Gallagher couldn't sleep that night either. Even passing her fifties, she was always a seductive and pretty woman. For the first time in thirty years, she spent a night without her husband or without the hope of seeing him again. At the time, everything was going so well. He was the only man of her life, and not once had she shown a true desire for another since she was seventeen years old. She had never imagined such a quick and heartbreaking ending. She felt lost. With the absence of Joyce, without Alison, she would be completely mislaid. She had many friends in Arab, but they were rather old-fashioned pies that were more affluent in gossip than in compassion. Moreover, she did have any doubt that they had circulated gossip on her back after the birth of Junior and Joyce's departure. So there was no question to become closer with them because they had always known that the true father of the child was a Black man. As for the friends of her late husband, she had never been close. It's a bunch of macho men who kept their wives like war trophies. She had the intention of freeing herself from this guardianship which cost her daughter so dearly.

To free her thoughts from the sadness caused by the emotions of the day, Mary Gallagher decided that from now on, Junior would sleep in her bed, at least until Joyce returned. She had also made the sublime gesture of giving a room in the house to all servants. They were related to the circumstances and the same emotions.

Late at night, while the little boy fell asleep in her bed, Mary called Ray. When she saw him again this morning, she had understood finally why her daughter had become madly in love. She also thought, she would have transcended racial issues into his arms. When the phone rang, she thought of hanging up, but eventually, she had taken her courage with both hands to engage in a conversation she did not know how to begin. To her wonder, it was easier than her beating heart tended to make him understand. They had therefore spent more than two hours to talk about various topics and make confessions to each other. If it wasn't for Junior's voice calling for his father, this conversation would have lasted a long time. She had never past as much time at phone with a man, not even with John at the time of the pre-wedding madness. She could not tell if she had been married for love or because it was her parents' choice. But she had never lived the passions of her daughter nor in the need to fight for something.

That gave a dull taste to its existence. It would take this tragedy and her concern of the moment to understand how she lacked many things in her life. Imagining her future, she thought she's going to put change to a lot of conventional habits, like getting out of this conformism south woman to embrace a new world that was developing in New York, Los Angeles, Chicago, etc. For this, she should begin, like her daughter, by defeating the barriers of this stuck society in which she had compiled so far.

CHAPTER 13
The Rough Way to Happiness

It would have taken more than two weeks to organize John Gallagher's funeral. During this period, Ray spent most of the time in Arab city. Mary Gallagher had wished that he began by making personal connections with Junior. He was now part of the family.

He met John and Mary's families for the first time that scattered everywhere in Georgia, Alabama, Mississippi, and South Carolina. They all returned to Arab for this occasion. They were part of a conservative network politician who controlled the political power, justice, and the business world in this part of the southern United States. The death of Gallagher was an opportunity to come together and strengthen the relationship.

Ray and Alison were the only Black people who were around John and Mary's families during this period. If for Alison the situation seemed normal because of her servant status, it was quite the opposite for Ray, which made the situation quite embarrassing most of the time. if it wasn't for the personality of Mary Gallagher and his love for Junior, Ray would already stop to come in this house. Mary and John's families were, in the beginning, even shocked by learning the links that united him to Joyce. But as they learned to know its history, behaviors had little by little changed. It was richer as each of them, as he was from a middle-class Christian parent, as he was a university graduate, a hero of the American army, former member of the DEA, and especially the savior of the family business that still made the pride of the Gallaghers and part of the region. With all this, the prejudices had diminished, and Alison had some pride in it. She just had her sixty years with forty years spent with the Gallaghers. She had even known John's grandfather. She knew, therefore, the manners and prejudices hidden. Seeing them, little by little, fussing with Ray made her happy.

Alison had also made sure that her story was known of this southern clan. She was married shortly before being hired by John's father. Then at the death of the latter, the son had insisted that she remain at his service and even going to find work for her husband in Arab. They were the only Black people who spent time at the Gallaghers. In fact, besides the servants who were not counted as part of the population, there were only a few non-Whites in this small town. When the need arose, John intervened to help her two children to have access to the white high school and later on to Alabama University. The two children were working now in Chicago and New York as a doctor and manager of a company. When her husband died, John Gallagher had done everything to relieve her and especially to convince her not to follow her children outside of Alabama. Since Junior's birth, she became the favorite friend of Mary Gallagher who treated her like as part of the family. She would be retired in two years by taking advantage of social security and some investments that John had made for her. Junior was her only concern, and he was like her grandson. She was the only Black person in Arab city that White people were accepting and sometimes took pleasure to see and converse with.

By learning the news of death of her father, Joyce or Sister Marie Anne was shattered. She hated him at the beginning of her arrival at Ixopo, and she cursed him even. But with her new religious education, prayer, and compassion gained by helping the poorest in the region, she had eventually acquired the Catholic devotion and forgiveness. She had felt the need to make peace with him. First of all, he was her father, and she was his princess. She could not consider him die at only fifty-five years. It would have taken the words of consolation from Sister Elizabeth and prayer of his religionists to be compliant of the reality. On leaving Ixopo, she travelled with a missal and a rosary as companions. She's concentrated in the prayer to forgive herself and have courage and the energy needed to deal with difficulties and the uncertainty that waited for her at Arab city. She knew that the next twenty-four hours would still be a tough test of her life.

Sister Marie Anne arrived at Montgomery Airport eight days after the death of her father. Being given the circumstances of her return to the United States of America and the malicious way they had arranged her release, the congregation director decided to travel with her. She was in her religious garb when she faced Roy at the airport exit. It was her who had been recognized as she was unrecognizable. The uniform had given her a rustic look as if she had not used beauty products in the last few months. She had the face soggy as if she had cried throughout the trip. She was no longer the cheerful and flippant young girl who made the young men of the university run. She was rather marked by a deep calm, soothing smile and almost asexual. She had become a true nun with an almost angel face. Seeing her walking slowly toward him with her little suitcase containing just the basic thing, a feeling of guilt passed through Roy. When she reached her height, she stopped her slow breath, paused, and skirted her right hand to indicate a distance descent between them. Then she turned her head to introduce Sister Elizabeth. After the thanks of use and the inspirited civilities, they took the direction of the highway without saying a word.

The highway leading to Arab city was completely clear. Both three made a low profile, not knowing how to start a conversation in a context where everyone had things to hide. It was Sister Elizabeth who broke the ice by interrogating Roy about the area. It was her first trip to the United States of America, and she was curious to learn things about customs in the south. Then there was a conversation between them throughout the ride. Sister Marie Anne pretended to sleep. She hadn't said a word in spite of the fact that she was challenged on various occasions. She reflected the way which she had to address the situation: Ray, her son, her father's funeral, and her future in the upcoming days. She had only questions and no certainty about how to perform. She was lost in her thought when the horn of the vehicle made her back. An old man who was at the viewpoint came to open the barrier. She recognized the seventy-year-old man who had seen her grow up. He looked like he was excited like a man in love. When Sister Marie Anne set foot on the ground, she had the surprise to see the employees from the house, Alison at their head, leaped toward her as if other people did not exist. They embraced her with a passion and warmth that ignored the hurdles that separated them. For the first times in months, she felt like and desire. She could not prevent to let the tears flow from happiness. She had never thought that these little people were also part of her family for worst or good. The spirit of hospitality had been replaced by a deep silence when Mary Gallagher came down the steps to walk toward. A trained domestic employee's hedge put her face-to-face to her daughter. Mary Gallagher, known for her coldness, threw herself in the arms of her daughter. The only words that came out of her mouth were to ask her forgiveness. This time, they were put to crying together with a fervor that did involve Sister Elizabeth and Alison to calm them down. "Thank you, my sister, for bringing my daughter back from Australia," Mary Gallagher said.

"My pleasure," Sister Elizabeth responded. "But instead, we come back from South Africa, in a small town called Ixopo."

Mary Gallagher looked at her guest with a glance of astonishment that said a lot about her ignorance. She turned her eyes to Sister Marie Anne with her nun uniform before returning to this one. "Anyway, thank you for taking care of her, and welcome at the house."

She took Roy's hand that she squeezed a little louder than usual as to express the rage of her heart and asked Sister Elizabeth to follow her. Roy kissed her on the forehead as a son would have done, and together, they took the way to the house, followed by the others.

Alison almost held up Sister Mary Anne that she came up to the house. She was clung to her when her mother had dropped her. She had her eyes closed and wet of tears. That's why she couldn't see this little boy standing in front of the entry room. It was his soft voice that bore Sister Marie Anne to open her eyes. She was immediately amazed. She fell to her knees before him, arms open. Junior hesitated before the impression made by the stranger with her religious dress. Then he flung himself on her knot without waiting for Alison's approving gesture. She was so strong that the child, in the end, told her that she smothered him. She released him to hold both his hands to better look him in the eyes without hiding the tears that began to flow this time. Junior wiped his eyes with his little fingers with childish tenderness and asked her if she was an angel. Sister

Marie Anne smiled gently, and he gave him two kisses before she said with a soft voice, "I am Sister Marie Anne." It was only then that she looked up to notice that the whole family of the mother's paternal side followed the scene. It was touching and frankly marvelous.

It was a reunification at the time, surprising and enjoyable. Sister Marie Anne did not expect that she would be filled with emotions as strong and pleasant. No member of the family was no longer expected to see her arrive in any suit. They eventually learned the mysteries surrounding the birth of Junior, as Mary Gallagher had explained everything, but seeing it happen this way followed by a nun was a shock unlikely. Finally, nobody had asked any questions at the moment. But everybody thought the reasons for this change by pasting the different pieces of the puzzle. In any case, it was a family matter, which would be discussed among family members at the right time.

When the courteousness was completed, Sister Marie Anne found her room for the first time since her banishment. It was all arranged in the same place she had left before her forced departure. It seemed that time had frozen in this place. Her father had insisted on this issue to the point of prohibiting access. She had caught also her childhood and her happy memories. Alison wasn't taking longer to find her with Junior in her arms. Until her mother could open her heart to talk to her about what was happening, Sister Marie Anne needed that a person made her part of the way which life was organized during her absence. She sat on the bed, and Sister Marie Anne curled up herself and let her head on Alison's thighs while Junior remained huddled on his mother. She stroked her hair, as she did the way in the past while she was telling history. It was at that point when Mary Gallagher opened the door to have the news of her daughter and fell on this scene of maternal intimacy that she would have wanted to be the main actress. She bit the lips of jealousy and prepared to close the door when Alison beckoned her to take the place. "It's up to you to talk to her," she said, with a bit of diplomacy that contrasted to what she started to do. Then she rose and made a gesture of the heart to explain to her how she supposed to talk to her daughter. She closed the door behind her, carrying Junior in her arms that plunged into a deep and happy sleep.

Mary Gallagher spent two hours head-to-head with her daughter. She told the whole story starting on her leaving Arab city until her return, which was organized without her knowledge. She confessed to her that she had engaged, in vain, without her husband's knowledge, a private detective to find her in Australia. It was only this morning that she had learned that she was in South Africa. She explained to her how Ray had saved her father from bankruptcy by applying the restructuring measures that she had proposed. Now the only thing she didn't know was about Ray's private life and what she intended to do with their son.

On the other hand, Sister Marie Anne told her the conditions of her exile at Ixopo and her life in this monastery in the midst of a population who were still living under an apartheid regime. "If 90 percent of the Blacks in this small town were like us, Arab city would be like a Gulag for Whites," she admitted to her mother. Ray's situation disturbed more than anything else. She could not say how she would react by seeing him again as long as she was in the uncertainty. For now, she hid behind her nun's clothes to suppress her feelings and also to avoid making illusions before the uncertainty of what her future and the upheavals that might have occurred in Ray's life during her absence. But the most troubling thing was the wonderful little boy who had changed her life and who anyway was an impediment in the pronunciation of her priestly vows. It would be to a lie to God and to the precepts of the Catholic Church to live this double life of renunciation of her responsibility of the mother and of false chastity. When her mother left the room, she reviewed her wardrobe. She had almost changed herself to put an end to this lie that everyone in her entourage was not tricked. But she revised and preferred to keep her habit of nun while waiting to find a way to deal with this dilemma. She should not be thrown into Ray's arms by seeing him again without knowing what had happened in his private life during her absence.

Having knowledge of Joyce/Sister Marie Anne's return, Ray stopped attending the Gallagher house. On the very day, he was yet in this property opposite to which now he wished to acquire. He returned two days later with the beautiful Lys Kay, an architect, and a construction firm. He wanted to make an assessment of the costs of repairs before making a final decision. Joyce was informed of his comings and goings and had spent the morning looking through the window to try to spot him. She did not want to call him knowing that he had voluntarily stopped attending the house as soon as he had learned her arrival. Her patience had paid off because she eventually noticed the movements on the property without being able to identify individuals. When she saw them go away, she lost all hope and immersed herself in an unintentional depression. As the hours passed without seeing Ray, the pressure took her away with a flame that burned her slowly from the inside. For once since the last few months, time seemed slow, painful, and unbearable. Bad thoughts tortured point, at a time, nightmares and erotic dreams.

The evening at the funeral home was no different. In spite of her immense grief, she had not been able to divert her mind of Ray. The tears that flowed from her eyes were more uncertainty than griefs for the loss of a loved one. She asked Roy to be informed of his absence, which he did without success. That evening was a torment. She hadn't closed her eyes like any other person in the house. She didn't expect as many sufferings. People around her also were impatient that it was over. Sorrow was real and unbearable.

The religious ceremony was scheduled at the First Arab Baptist Church at 7:00 a.m. and the burial three hours later at the Cemetery Memorial. Everything had started at the time planned. Almost every adult in this little town counted were present in more than fifty VIP from Montgomery and Washington, DC. Senators, congressmen, businessmen, judges, mayors, student delegations from the city and University of Alabama, and many little Arab people were present to pay respect to this man who had so marked lives in this part of the south. The church was full, and most of people followed the ceremonies outside. Fortunately, the pastor had installed giant screens and speakers. It was a sober moment and filled with emotions. The solidarity with the Gallaghers was sincere and full of compassion. When the coffin crossed the door of the church, a round of applause rang out. They kept clapping until the convoy disappeared from the sights. The procession to the cemetery was slow and silent. Cars and people were lined up along the road. Eyes were fixed on the family van, hoping to see the face of the little boy who did fail the heart of John Gallagher to the point that he carried him to make the ultimate sacrifice of his life to save him. That day, a thought flashed through the Arab population to know love was stronger than discrimination.

The burial ceremonies were also a moment filled with strong emotions. The audience had made a huge circle around the tomb to listen to the last prayers and the touching last speech of the oldest brother of John Gallagher. The pastor gave the final blessing, and the coffin was slipped slowly into the cellar under the wet eyes and the complaints contained in the audience. Then the family members, followed by the assistants, dropped a handful of roses before dispersing slowly. Small groups all over the cemetery stayed for a short time to discuss before going to the Gallaghers' home for gathering.

Sister Marie Anne was even more anxious in finding that Ray was not in the church. She was so preoccupied with his absence that she had heard very little of the warm words intended for her during the whole ceremony. It was also the same thing at the cemetery. When it was time to go back into the limo to get home, she saw herself approaching two couples from her father's tomb, among which a man holding in his left hand a red rose. She stopped a moment to better identify latecomers. She felt that the latter were doing their best to avoid whether they were identified. As they got closer, the shadows of Ray, his parents, and a pretty woman whom she didn't know were more visible. Suddenly, her heart began to drum vehemently. She had failed to move toward them, but she knew she wouldn't have the courage to learn in this circumstance that Ray was so quickly comforted in the arms of another as elegant with the approval of his parents. She had preferred to turn her head and tapped the shoulders of the driver to tell him to drop her home. She got the idea that this woman was the true motive for his absence. She then immersed himself in a melancholy even deeper than that caused by his exile and the death of her father.

The residence of Mary Gallagher was filled by family members, friends from Montgomery, and sympathizers living at Arab city. They were all over the courtyard, on the veranda, in the boudoir, and same on the floors. Politicians, policemen, magistrates, businessmen, and ordinary citizens mixed and took advantage to discuss in enjoying the catering committed by the citizens of the city and the city hall. It was a way to demonstrate their recognition toward this family that was beating partly the heart of Arab city. Sister Marie Anne, like other members of the family, was everywhere to greet and thank people. Some took advantage to make a brief mostly at the young woman with a nun robe that seemed to escape from some extremist Muslim country. She had a platter of glasses of lemonade in hand, crossing the boudoir because she was going to serve a group of children who were playing with Junior when she heard behind her, repeating the deep solemn voice, "My sister." She stopped immediately, petrified as if she had lost most of her capabilities. She dropped the platter without realizing it, and drinks sank down. She turned her head mechanically, scared and confused mind to deal with Ray, his parents, and the young woman accompanying him. It was more than heartbreaking but frankly demeaning and unfair, she thought. She breathed slowly trying to remain calm despite the too intensive beats of her heart to look up at Ray who set eyes with a slight smile and surprise to see her dressed as if she were part of a cult "Hi, Ray," she told him. And they remained to look in the eyes without moving and without knowing what to start. Finally, it was Marie Louise Gaillard, dragging her husband by the hand, who approached her with a zest that contrasted with the suspicions of the young religious. She warmly embraced her without worrying about her dress that she believed to be a kind of self-punishment that she had inflicted her. She had made the remark in a pleasant way when Jonathan went in turn to greet her. Marie Louise Gaillard was congratulated in having her back and dared to say that this time, she shouldn't stray too far for too long. Meanwhile, Lys Kay disappeared. She was a businesswoman. She realized that there were important people that she had to meet, so she was everywhere, taking advantage of her charm to engage in brief conversations and exchange business cards.

Sister Marie Anne and the Gaillards spoke for about twenty minutes about everything and especially the tragic death of John Gallagher. Despite herself, she had to invent a more playful story about this nun habit without going into the details of her departure from the United States or of her internment forced in South Africa. It was a surprise! Ray was dismayed, as he had found this modesty in the eyes of Joyce who seemed to assert herself as good faith. Despite everything, he made a malicious joke about her outfit. Knowing his playful spirit, she smiled too meaningful that her pious lie had worked. The arrival of Mary Gallagher put an end to this exchange not without leaving Sister Marie Anne with the question that burned her heart.

The Gaillards met Mary Gallagher for the first time with confidence and simplicity. They switched regular niceties for the occasion. The mother of Sister Marie Anne seemed touched to learn that the couple made the trip to Florida to come to the funeral. The Gaillards spoke English properly and expressed with the emphasis strongly marked by the French. That charmed Mary Gallagher, and she made the comment with kindness and good curiosity. And, of course, a good feeling agreed between the two women. She wanted to know more about them and to talk also to them about the complexity of the situation! So she invited Jonathan and his wife in the boudoir for a private conversation. Before she went away, she called a maid to clean the floor and apologized to Ray and Joyce without worrying about their slightest.

The heart of Sister Marie Anne had become to throb again as was finally happened the proper time to satisfy her curiosity more than stifling. Her anxiety was substantial as much as the bad feelings of Ray in front of this fake nun.

"Then, my dear nun, since I don't know your religious name yet, you look very bronzed like you want to be closer to Haitian people."

But she had heard nothing of this joke. The only thing that interested her really was that lady with blue eyes she had seen at the cemetery. Jealousy worried her at point that let her sputtering. Then unable to continue to distress themselves, she addressed the question directly to him, "Who is she?" "Who is who?" he murmured, Ray faking goodness.

"The lady that go together with you?"

"Ah," said Ray, "you mean Lys Kay." He resumed, "It should always be there. You want that I present to you," he replied by turning his head, pretending to look for her.

It looked like he did it on purpose. Seeing that the explanations were slow in coming, she decided to turn her back in a barely contained rage. Ray slightly pulled the sleeve of her dress to stop her.

"Sorry, my sister! She is a realtor that my financial agent, Brian Donovan, had hired to help me buy a house."

Then taking a serious tone this time, Ray explained to her how Brian Donovan had convinced him to buy the property opposite and that, by accident, he was on his first visit when the fire had declared itself to Alison's apartment. He explained the events in detail, downhearted, as if John Gallagher were his friend. She took his hand and looked at him with a sad face when he explained her father's sacrifice to save Junior. Their eyes encountered as if the touch of the hand had born a spark. Ray was silent and was penetrated by the sparkling eyes of Joyce. A thrill passed through them, and if it was not for the decorum they had always demonstrated, they would have been in the arms of the other. Then Joyce jumped as if she'd just waken up brutally. She stood up and turned her back from Ray rushing into her room.

Mary Gallagher and the Gaillards, observing the scene, couldn't prevent to question the defiance of Sister Marie Anne. During their first meet, they were agreed to put together in order to convince the young woman to leave fall that dress that made elsewhere gossiping everyone because the secret to the birth of Junior was right now known to everyone. And then John's death precipitated the need to solve this annoying problem for the family. Mary Gallagher was too proud of her to continue to live this lie that her husband had imposed on her. Then they went up in the room of Sister Marie Anne to reason with her. For her mother, her daughter couldn't believe that after a sexual life also intense and also filled with a child as a reward that she would pass quietly the rest of her life in asceticism and oblivion. She did wrongly understand the words of St. Paul.

Arriving in front of Sister Marie Anne's room, Mary Gallagher struck three blows. She had not expected a response to push the door. The few minutes she had spent with her new allies had opened her eyes to a world that she was unaware. Now they had become accomplices. Besides, Ray's control on the family business had already permanently soldered links.

Upon entering the room, the trio found Sister Marie Anne lying on the bed in the fetal position and her small suitcase well done in a corner. She had decided to resume the plane before the date scheduled for her return, fleeing Arab and her fear. She was unsure and confused between her deep feelings for her son, for Ray, and acquired religious faith after the trauma that she generated her forced exile and fundamentalism with which made her swallow the conservative religious precepts. She eventually accepted in her moments of solitude at Ixopo could not trust that in God because nobody was able to bring her back in the United States of America after the betrayal by the person she believed to be her true princess. But she was being held so far by an inner strength that she could not tame.

"But what is happening to you, my daughter?" Marie Louise Gaillard tenderly told her as she rushed up to her to take her in her arms. Once attached to her, Sister Marie Anne broke into tears.

"Jonathan Gaillard, you'll wait outside," said his wife. The latter did not repeat it twice. He left the room as if he was escaping jail. He had always been uncomfortable in the presence of women in tears. When he slammed the door behind him, Mary Gallagher rushed to turn toward the bed. She took her daughter in her arms to hug her very strongly. Then she began to cry also. Marie Louise Gaillard left them for a few minutes because both had good reasons to be sad. Then she brought them back to reality. As she did that, Sister Marie Anne removed the head. She could be real religious for the rest of her life.

Marie Louise Gaillard and Mary Gallagher used their life experiences to speak to Sister Marie Anne of her real situation. They made her understand that she was a victim, certainly an injustice, but that it was time to draw a line under the past and turn her life around. They explained to her that even her father, before his death, had expressed a desire to do what was necessary to be forgiven. So she couldn't deprive, especially her son, of his mother's affection. It was her responsibility to take care of Junior. They planned to talk to Sister Elizabeth to close the chapter.

Sister Marie Anne gave the impression of having agreed to the advice of the two women and even tried a discreet smile to reassure them. She wiped her eyes and apologized for being so childish. She asked them, however, to let her, until tonight, the time to put an order in her mind. "By tomorrow morning," she said, "I will end up really starting to mourn this and embrace the life that awaits me." She asked Marie Louise Gaillard to apologize to Ray, as she wanted now to be alone without any psychological compulsion to meditate. The presence of the father of her son disturbed her to the point that she was unable to be lucid. With that, the two women gave her a kiss on the forehead and turned away. They were thankful to have been able to convince her to not make a mistake she could regret later.

Ray went home dubiously. He believed that Sister Marie Anne would be delighted to resume living together with him. He could not imagine the depth of the trauma caused by her exile in Ixopo. He was unable to understand that inside the young woman battled the faith in an environment of religious asceticism and a sensual yet unfulfilled desire. He was angry with himself for having waited for a woman who really didn't want him anymore. Maybe, he thought, she regretted having been seduced by a Black. After all, she could be like her father, racist and nasty. He was already wary by the reassuring words from his mother. Now in the solitude of his room, after many reflections, he decided to stop buying the Arab property while the process was already well underway and leave the south forever. He would decide soon on his new destination far from the White fanatics of Montgomery.

It was seven o'clock in the morning when Alison climbed the stairs to bring breakfast to Sister Marie Anne in her bed. Mary Gallagher and Sister Elizabeth went together to the church as two good friends. As in the past, every time she wanted to spoil her, she made her favorite food and served her in bed. She took no time to knock and pushed the door of the room. It was always her little girl, she never did formality. She was always protesting after her puberty, but she didn't give any attention to that. Joyce had occupied a single room since her four years, and Alison had always made the same thing. It was not today that she was going to change. And as usual, she left voluntarily her voice to greet her a long and happy song. But when her eyes fell on the bed, she could not retain her surprise and scream. "My God, what happened to my little girl?" Indeed, she noted with amazement that the bed was well done, the room well arranged, and the small suitcase not in its usual place. She searched everywhere, in rooms, in vain. She went down the stairs to run talk to the staff of the house. But no one had seen her out. Half an hour later, after being convinced of the real absence of Sister Marie Anne, Alison took the initiative to call the police chief. She was driving by the gardener to pick Mrs. Gallagher. She couldn't wait for her return.

Fortunately, Mary Gallagher was still on the porch of the church in great conversation. Seeing her arrive, she knew something was wrong. So she walked to Alison to ask her the question. She explained the absence of Sister Marie Anne and trying not to panic her. They surrendered immediately to the police station to meet the chief. The latter called Montgomery's FBI chief to seek his help. He was a friend, and he knew John Gallagher well. The result was immediate. Indeed, he found the trace of a ticket bought by Joyce Gallagher for a trip to South Africa and a shot of phone calls made from a public booth in the Airport de Montgomery. The flight was intended at 12:00 p.m. toward New York with different transit by land at Durban the next day. Mary Gallagher called immediately the Gaillards so that they would go to Montgomery Airport quickly to hold her until her arrival. Arab city police chief, especially, asked Detective David Kennedy to go together with Mary Gallagher in order to reach the destination before the departure of the aircraft, as time was running out. He allowed him to use an undercover police vehicle with emergency privileges. The Gaillards arrived at the airport first and immediately proceeded to the boarding gate. But to their astonishment, the plane was already headed on the flight ramp. It was with the face filled with bitterness that they saw their last hope go away. The hardest part would be to inform Ray. He would not come.

When Ray picked up the phone at his house, he was already in great anxiety. He expected his mother to tell him that Sister Marie Anne would not listen to them and that she had taken the plane to return to South Africa. So he had not reacted when he learned that the plane had left the door thirty minutes earlier in his schedule and that she was unable to talk to her. A short silence reigned on the phone. Neither one nor the other could not find words to express their disenchantment. "I'm sincerely sorry, my son," repeated Marie Louise Gaillard. "We are all here."

"Maybe it's better like that," replied Ray. "Don't worry, Mom, I'll survive to that. Request Mary Gallagher to join me at the restaurant at 7:00 p.m. I invite you all." Then he hung up.

The Best Frenchie was the only restaurant that Ray constantly attended since arriving in Montgomery.

Each time, he would sit at the same table to the point where he eventually attracted the attention of the manager. For employees, he was part of the house. His manners, his presence, and his almost theatrical gaze had charmed even other regular customers. One day, a pretty White woman approached him to make him known there was something in his manner which was not quite American. He smiled in noting that there was curiosity. He responded with a bit of humor to entrust to the lady that his Americanness improved with the colorful culture of Haiti. And the lady was graced with a broad smile before living. Since then, they had become friends.

That night, before arriving at the restaurant, he had called to reserve a table for eight people by counting his parents, Alison, Junior, Mary Gallagher, and the policeman. It was Brian who had advised him this restaurant because the boss was a former commando of Operation Eagle Claw, who was to release the hostages of the American Embassy in Tehran in April 1980. After the failure of the mission, he had retired and had reverted as a chief cooker. When he had learned that Ray was attending his institution, he had formally asked the supervisor to do everything to satisfy his every desire in order to avoid especially that no discriminatory act was committed toward him. He knew enough about this city to predict that a far-right employee could afford a gap which would cause irreparable damage.

The group met as agreed without a good soul. It was not a joyful encounter, and the conversation was slow to start. To forget the disappointments of the day, Ray had requested that attention be concentrated on the memory of John Gallagher. Soon after the funeral, we should not forget him already. Mary Gallagher smiled at the idea that it was the man who was responsible for all his problems that Ray wished to honor the memory. It must be believed that the heroic gesture that he had consented to save Junior's life much moved the military that he was, beyond even the controversies that divided them.

The manager of the restaurant had come in person, this time to welcome Ray and his guests. At this time, the restaurant was full of only White customers, as it was most of the time. He took the opportunity to present his condolences to Mary Gallagher which he knew the husband of name and reputation. But what was most interesting was Ray himself because his reputation as former military and American hero was well known in the restaurant.

Standing around the table and in the twilight, the manager discussed in low voice with Ray and his guests. What frankly had contributed to decrease the bad soul, he did not realize that the lady who had just stood beside them was not that of a worker who wanted to take the orders. Yet all customers staring at the eyes of this nun were a little embarrassed that she did not know how to say even hello. Finally, taking her courage with both hands, she let out the two simplest words "Good evening." She stood with her long dress and little suitcase at her hand. Inadvertently, she was facing Ray when he turned around to identify the voice behind him. If the manager had returned politeness immediately, it was not so much for others. They were left speechless. But Sister Marie Anne had already ignored them, including Junior who was struggling with a toasty. She stared Ray right in the eyes as if nothing else existed around. She had felt her mind foggy and his body on fire. She was unable to decide what to say or do in this moment. The charm was so strong that she didn't know at what moment she plunged on Ray to kiss him in a long kiss that seemed to last all the time they were deprived one another. Then she clung at him very strongly, her head bent over his shoulder to let the last tears flow, which let go her wretched story forever.

The surprise was just as much for the restaurant manager as the guests before the strangeness of the image of that White nun who kissed a Black man in the middle of a restaurant frequented by White people among the most conservative of this southern region of the Deep South states. "We need another chair," said the waitress who had finally brought herself. She had the air ravished the bold scene. She was an emancipated young White girl who was studying at the University of Alabama and who had already lost the complexes of old White people by flirting with Black players at the basketball team.

Mary Gallagher was delighted. It was her who pulled Sister Marie Anne in Ray's arms to tighten against her with a rare maternal fervor before allowing Alison the time to calm her touchiness. Then it was a chain of hugs and whispers that troubled the tranquility of the restaurant. It seemed like the attraction kept all eyes in a joyful spirit. For the time being, everybody forgot about John Gallagher. The spirits were elsewhere, far from the sorrows caused by his death. Mary took the ingenuity, this time, by asking the accompanying detective to pick up the little bag she had in the trunk of the car and bring it to the women toilets. Before going away with her daughter, she said to her guests with a rare feature of humor, "That Sister Marie Anne had just resigned from her function of nun." A subtle laughter went throughout the restaurant. Then the manager went to fetch his best bottle of wine as a gift to Ray to celebrate the return of happiness.

Joyce spent fifteen minutes in the bathroom with her mother. When all was done, Mary Gallagher had hidden furtively to let her daughter take the way back alone. Fortunately, she instinctively regained her spontaneous effect of stylishness. Ultimately, she was a converted woman who walked across the restaurant. This time, the guests were charmed. It looked like a straight exit Photoshop of an issue of the Vanity Fair magazine. In less time, Mary Gallagher had been done of Sister Marie Anne, the grim nun, a sensual and youthful young woman. Seeing her arrive, Ray stood up to go and greet her. But also everyone around the table had risen. The gesture of admiration was way beyond the table. Like a good gentleman, Ray pulled out the chair for her to sit at his side. She looked like a shy girl who had just returned from the den of uninhibited sexuality.

Before arriving at dinner, Ray asked the waitress to bring his special order. At the same time, he asked Junior to close his eyes. Everyone was far from remembering this week that the little boy had just been three years old. When he laid the cake with her three candles, Junior was in the angels. "Happy birthday, John Gallagher Junior Gaillard," he said. "Your gift, you'll get it at home." On this, he took him in his arms and lifted him up to be between him and Joyce. And the two of them gave him a kiss on his cheeks.

Mary Gallagher moved toward them, kissed Junior in her turn, and told him as she looked at him in his eyes, "My little Junior, I'm sensing your real mother Joyce and your true father Ray. I'm just the grandmother." Then it was the Gaillards' turn to introduce themselves to the little boy as also his grandparents. Junior let himself go of all his emotions by clinging to Joyce and in rewarding her with a long kiss. When it was time to sing "Happy Birthday," it was the waitresses and some curious clients who spontaneously joined the celebration that Junior blew his three candles.

It was in the kindliness of this improvised atmosphere that the idea grew instinctively into Ray's thinking. Without even taking the time to think, he let himself be guided by the warmth that ignited his heart. So even before people stopped singing, he knelt in front of Joyce. It would have taken time that they noticed his gesture. The voices immediately became quiet. Curiosity and suspense blocked the glances that launched absolutely from a man who was on the verge of making his request. Before he had time to speak, Junior insisted on getting off the arms of his mother. With the goodness and spontaneity of a happy child, he knelt beside his father, arms outstretched to Joyce. A sublime laugh of men's voices echoed through the room while the wet eyes of the women claimed handkerchiefs. Then with apparent calmness, Ray repeated as in a poem:

> Time has freed itself from heartbreaking passion and social
> constraints; the heart has completely healed from the stagnate of
> the painful separation.
> The time has come for man to embrace his future and to the
> woman to enjoy the happiness she deserved. I am my father's
> way without you, she will be lost in the mazes of uncertainty,
> loneliness and monotony.
> Do you want to be the light on my way, the
> look that will appreciate the colors of life
> and the sun that will warm my eternity; do
> you want to be my other half?

Joyce, eyes wet because of tears, knelt also before the two men of her life, and even before she said a word, Junior took both hands to join them together. And in a fervent impulse, he repeated, "I pronounce you my father and my mother. So, Dad, you can kiss Mom." It was still an outburst of joy. Definitely, he was really his father's son. He had a bright future ahead of him.

What was to be something simple and banal became an explosion of joy as a scent of happiness went through the restaurant. But Ray, still stoic, drew from his finger the same engagement ring he had offered to Sarah Altieri to slide in Joyce's finger, waiting to do better. The audience applauded, and a festive moment settled in the restaurant. Hand in hand, Joyce and Ray rose up at the moment when Jonathan Gaillard made his toast. This time, it was in a conscious way that Joyce threw in Ray's arms for the rewarding kiss that lit up the room. Unanimous applause rose immediately to congratulate the couple. And in the wake of the atmosphere, feelings woke up. Thus, they had never seen so many couples kissing in one shot in an American restaurant. Only the Gaillards made the economy. The Haitian's traditionalists did not kiss in public and should not be too much to annoy also Mary Gallagher at a time like this.

The light of the camera of the manager from the restaurant brought Joyce and Ray at reality. Then he asked them to position themselves to make other pictures some with Junior, some with the Gaillards or even with couples from the restaurant who asked, etc. When it was the turn of Gaillard and Gallagher family, Mary had the surprise to see David Kennedy, the fifty-five-year-old detective, hold her hand so close. In the spontaneity of the gesture and the feel of the environment, she didn't react. But when Kennedy had become closer to the point of brushing the breast crease that made her startled, she turned to him surprised and amazed at the audacity. Instead of protesting, she gave him a shining smile. The police officer smiled gently and passed her hand over Mary's belt before telling her, whispering, "I live alone."

ABOUT THE AUTHOR

Raynand Pierre—lawyer, journalist, and human rights activist—was born in Saint-Michel-de-l'Attalaye (Haiti) in 1960. He is the son of a former mayor and planter and a conservative Catholic teacher. He began campaigning in the League of Human Rights in 1978 and then in various organizations, including the League for the Defense of Children's Rights, of which he was a founding member and president in 1986. He became secretary general of the Centre for the Promotion of Human Rights in 1988 and Secretary General of the National Confederation of Educators of Haiti (CNEH) in 2000. He has worked for more than twenty years for various United Nations missions and NGOs. He has collaborated with several magazines specializing in human rights issues and the daily newspaper Le Nouvelliste. He taught history for more than five years.

BLURB

Ray Gaillard was an American born of Haitian origin who served in the famous Navy Seal, under cover of United States Agency for International Development (USAID) but worked, in fact, for Drug Enforcement Administration (DEA) in the past two years.

At twenty-four, Joyce Gallagher was a happy and truthfully pretty young lady. At this age, she still hadn't had a boyfriend, an unusual thing for a young girl having passed already six years in university.

The Gaillard family was part of a greater Catholic traditional caste that occupied the highest functions of that little city in Haiti. It was also an ancestry of large landowners that benefited from the generosity of the different governments.

The Gallagher family was part of an old traditional White conservative origins from Ireland who had made their fortune first in the slave trade and then in the processing of food products.

What do you expect when the only child of a White supremacist family from the Deep South of America fell in love with a Black son of an immigrant family from a broken country?